Diary

A

Care Assistant

Written by Roseanne Webb

Contents

Introduction   **5**

Gratitude   **7**

One   **13**

Two   **28**

Three   **47**

Four   **72**

Five   **86**

Six   **100**

Seven   **109**

Eight   **126**

Nine   **147**

Ten   **181**

Introduction

This book has been written by an ex Domiciliary Care Assistant, whose sole purpose in writing it, is to give insight into the world of the Care system, and to show what it is really like to work in its front line.

The author wishes to bring a smile to fellow Care Workers who will relate to it, and also to show how challenging the role can be to others.

All characters are entirely fictional. Any resemblance to real people or circumstances are entirely coincidental.

Based on a true story.

Gratitude

Thank you to all of my clients who inspired me to write this, and taught me so much. You all deserve to get the best out of life, and I wish you all well.

Thank you to my fellow Care Workers who trained me, talked with me, bitched with me and kept me sane through it all. Your dedication and commitment has not gone unnoticed. One day, the government will hopefully notice it too, and reward you all with that much needed and deserved pay rise!

Thank you to my partner, my friends and family for putting up with me being antisocial while I wrote this, and for your help, guidance, and patience.

Lots of love,

Roseanne x

Diary of a Care Assistant

Just like anybody else in the working world, some days I enjoy my job. On other days, I don't.
For example, on good days, I feel humbled and joyous that what I do for a living is enabling others to live their lives easier, remain as independent as possible, and ensure that my clients get some sort of familiar and friendly contact with another human being and the outside world on a daily basis, and I feel good about it.
On other days, I resent my alarm clock waking me up to signal that it is yet again time to leave my glorious duvet cocoon to head out into the elements, drive around in all weathers all day, have the same conversations, clean up someone else's cabbage scented shit whilst discussing the latest news or a soap opera for the fifteenth time that day, on less than five hours of sleep, picking up less than minimum wage, and going home to the same arguments about money, vehicle repairs, growing debts, running myself mentally, physically, emotionally and financially into the ground for the sake of the same job, and screaming with my partner about the fact that I'm never there, and when I am, I am so exhausted and drained that I may as well not be.

Welcome to the world of a Domiciliary Care Assistant

AKA Community Care Worker, Health Care Assistant (HCA), Care Worker, Support Worker, and various other titles.

Regardless of job title, the work is generally the same.
In short, duties vary with each client but can include (and not limited to): washing and bathing clients, helping them to dress/undress, prepare meals, administer medication, provide domestic help like cleaning, laundry and shopping, help filling in forms and managing finances, making appointments and escorting clients to them, providing companionship through talking and listening, liaising with family, friends and health care professionals.
All the general things that most people do for themselves without even having to think about it.
And all within a 30 minute slot.

One thing this job has taught me is to never take anything for granted.
I often go about my daily duties and think to myself, that this may well be me when I am older.
I may be all alone, probably with some cats, having some overworked and underpaid exhausted care workers looking after me, my only contact with the outside world being 15-30 minutes, 3-4 times a day.
I just hope that the pay and working conditions are better for the workers by then, else I'll end up with some emotionally drained, pissed off nineteen year old, struggling to make ends meet, knackered, rushing to get all

of their jobs done, no time to talk or sit down and share a cuppa with me.

Some of my clients have their care funded by Social Services, and it costs the government a fortune.
Some of my clients pay privately for their care, and it costs them or their families a fortune.
Regardless of who pays, all clients receive the same standard of care, and neither I nor my colleagues ever see this 'fortune'.
We get paid minimum wage, but only for the actual time spent with each client. The time spent traveling between each client visit (anything between 5-30 minutes) is not paid. We get 17p per mile, which does not cover the fuel costs on the average car, let alone wear and tear, tyres, servicing etc, which is why I use a motorcycle instead.
We have an aging population, requiring more assistance and a growing demand in care services, but with funding cuts, the care system has become a national crisis.
More people are needing care than ever, and there simply are not enough care workers to meet the demand.

My colleagues and I do our best.
We get crap pay, not enough time to complete our work, not enough sleep, and we struggle to get the necessities done for our clients, like showers, shaves, serve a hot meal, all whilst struggling to put food on our own tables.
But I still go in to each client with a warm smile, and chat away whilst I wash and dry my clients, apply creams, change their

incontinence pads and wipe up any mess, because I understand that my clients are just as human as me, and I will age just like them, and I may require some help one day, just like them.

I understand that I may be the only person that they see each day, and so if I am rushed, stressed, tired, skint and bloody hungry, it doesn't matter - because it's about them, not me.

They deserve a warm smile and an ear to their troubles.

And so us care staff do all of our own complaining on the brief 2-5 minutes between calls if we happen to be with another colleague, and we happen to get the chance to talk, and we go home crying with exhaustion, and take out the stresses of our day to our partners, husbands and wives.

We are Shift Workers.
We work days, nights, weekends, bank holidays, even Christmas day.
On our rare days off we get bombarded with phone calls begging us to work a shift, or half a shift, or just two client calls, as someone's off sick, someone's car has broken down, everyone's running late, someone wants directions to the client out at the farm in the middle of nowhere, someone can't find a client's medication, the care plan is missing, etc

Like doctors and nurses, our profession is 24/7, 365 days of the year, and it is one of the toughest jobs I have ever had.

One

My alarm shrieks at 5am, making me jump as I struggle to unravel my bed covers to free my hands to turn the damn thing off.
Pete stirs beside me, and gets up to put the kettle on whilst I head to the bathroom to wash, wee, brush my teeth, get dressed, sort my hair out and attempt to look alive.
I force a smile in the mirror, but it looks more like a grimace, so I quickly lose it and head to the kitchen to drink the coffee that my lovely man has kindly made for me.
I thank him, kiss him, and head outside to finish this delightful cup of caffeine and have a cigarette.
Pete has kindly made me a flask full of coffee ready to take, along with some cereal bars.
I now have a large stash of cereal bars in my bag because I never get a bloody chance to eat them.
Pete starts up my motorcycle for me whilst I check my work phone's app to see where I am first on the rota.
(Our work phones do not work as actual phones, as they do not make or receive calls, but do have a tracking device so that the office can spy on you to see where you are).
I will be spending most of my 16 hour day in Staffordshire, around Penkridge, Wheaton Aston, Bishops Wood, Brewood, and then one random call in Wolverhampton.
My rota is back to back calls all day as the office haven't allowed for any time between

clients, and so I calculate how late I will be running as I put my ciggy out and light another.

I will be approximately 1 hour and 40 minutes late by 1pm, where the first half of my shift should end. The second half starts at 4pm and should end at 10pm, however it will be about 11.30pm by the time I arrive home.

I have decided that I hate the office staff and their shitty rotas.

Start at 6am, get home for midnight, followed by the same tomorrow, and the next day.

In between, we're supposed to shower, eat, and sleep.

Yep.

That's a really healthy way to live.

That's really safe for the clients, having half asleep care staff administering medication and driving around country lanes in the dark.

What could possibly go wrong there?

Bastards, with their 9-5 roles, and access to a kettle, and a toilet.

Grr.

I kiss Pete goodbye, and set out on my half hour journey to my first call.

It is a double up call, meaning two care workers are required for the client.

I'm 10 minutes early, so I park up and head round the corner to smoke a quick cigarette before my double up partner arrives, and sip coffee from my flask, watching the early morning cars going past as I daydream.

My partner arrives, and it is Sue, the Care Coordinator.

I like Sue. She's not everybody's cup of tea, but I find her funny because she's very upfront about how much she resents the company and management, and swears a lot - not in front of clients, I might add, but outside of work there's been many a time that we've sat in an all-night trucker's cafe after shift, tired, angry and broken, eating chips and all day breakfasts, drinking coffee and slagging off the managers and their lack of managing before heading home to sleep.

"Morning Rose," she says, getting out of her car, looking severely pissed off as usual.

"Hi Sue, you alright?" I ask, walking up the client's path to the bungalow.

"Am I alright? Am I fuck! This is supposed to be my day off. My one day off in like, three weeks. And then someone phoned in sick. And Sarah doesn't give a shit, so she told me I have to cover the shift. So here I am, on my one day off, at fucking work."

Sue gets the key from the key safe.

"Shit, but I thought Sarah was on call this weekend?" I say to her.

"So did I, but here I am. Sarah won't come out. The manager won't come out now that she has me to do all her work for her!" she grumbles.

"I guess your promotion to coordinator isn't going too well for you, huh?"

"No, it isn't going well, Rose. I hate this fucking company."

Sue puts the key in the lock, and we step inside.

"Good morning, Gladys!" we cheerily call out in unison.

"Morning, girls!" Gladys calls back.

We go in to her, all smiles, chatting away as we assist her out of the bed, into the wheelchair, into the bathroom, take out her incontinence pad, and give her some privacy. Sue and I head into the kitchen where Sue writes out the care notes in the care plan folder, and I whip up a bowl of cornflakes with milk, a cup of tea and a glass of water.
I pop it all in the lounge for her and put the news on the television ready, then make the bed, open all the curtains, put the stand aid in front of the chair, take the rubbish out, then rejoin Sue while we wait for Gladys to call us back in.
Sue closes the folder and yawns.
"How much sleep did you get last night?" I ask her.
"Not enough!" she laughs, "about four hours. You?"
"Five. Got in at eleven last night, showered, beans on toast for tea, went to bed at midnight, then up at five this morning."
"It's shit, ay it?" she says, "they've took on too many clients, overworking the staff, so everyone keeps leaving, and even the new staff are leaving! One started last month, worked one shift, then sent in a doctors note for stress at work. She's gone now." Sue tells me.
"One shift was too much for her, then!" I say, and laugh.
"I'm surprised you haven't left, to be honest," she says.

"Mate, I'm too knackered to even look for a new job!"
We both start laughing, then Gladys calls us back.

"What are you pair giggling about?" Gladys asks, as we wash and dry her back.
"It's Sue telling me rude jokes again!" I tell her.
"No I didn't, Gladys, Rose is telling lies again!" Gladys chuckles, and we help her to get dressed, then take her into the lounge to her chair, and pass her the tray with her breakfast on.
"What was the rude joke, then?" Gladys asks as we put our coats on, "come on, give an old girl a laugh!"
Sue whispers something in her ear which sets her off giggling.
"Right girls, you can clear off now! What time are you pair back later?" Gladys asks.
"We've got you down for 11.30, but we might be a bit late," I tell her.
"Well, please get here before one o'clock, because yesterday the girls were nearly two hours late, and I was desperate for the loo, and when they got here, I was in a right mess!" she says.
"We'll do our best, Gladys, we'll keep you updated," Sue says, and we head off.
Sue and I both have some single calls before our next double up. I head one way, Sue heads the other.

My next call is only five minutes away, and I go in ten minutes early.

I always try and get the morning calls out of the way as fast as possible, so that I can make up time in the afternoon.

It sounds bad, that I want them out of the way, but if I am to provide any kind of almost reasonable service, I need to rearrange my rota and cut the calls down if I can. If I followed my rota as it is laid out, and spent the whole allocated time with all clients, I would always be running 2 hours + late.

On my rota today, there are only two 'time specific' clients. One, who complained and complained to the company director about never seeing the same carer more than twice, and not being able to have a routine or make plans due to carers turning up early or late and never on time, and the other who has an evening call which must be on time due to being administered warfarin.

The others don't really mind as long as you aren't more than half an hour early or late, and if you are late, they like a phone call from the office.

The office staff don't usually phone clients, though. They're much too busy phoning carers begging them to cover shifts.

I go into my next call, to a lady who loves gardening and flowers. I chat away to her about my trouble with the climbing roses, and talk about my winter flowering Heather plants doing well as I get her washed and dressed, apply her creams and make her breakfast. She offers tips about digging bonemeal around the root ball of my roses and we discuss the large crop of pears she had from her garden this autumn.

I scribble notes in the care plan folder and leave five minutes early.

My next call is an elderly gentleman in a supported living complex. This is supposed to be a half hour call, but he tends to get himself up, washed and dressed before the care workers arrive, so I can usually get him sorted in fifteen minutes.

I empty his catheter bag, attach it onto his leg with two straps, and dispose of the night bag, then walk with him to his girlfriend's flat a few doors down.

We also care for his girlfriend, so once he's seated, I sort out the lady's eye drops, put her hearing aids in, and make them both a coffee. She has made breakfast for them both prior to my arrival, so once I've scribbled my notes, I leave them both in peace.

I have managed to shorten down two calls of a combined 45 minutes, into 25 minutes.

If I hadn't cut these calls short, I would be running late to my next double up with Sue, and then we would both be running late.

I head to my next double up with Sue, to a gentleman who has had a stroke. His is an hour's call, but we usually get him done under 40 minutes.

Sue jumps out of her car, and stamps out her cigarette as I arrive, and the client's wife lets us in.

"Morning Debbie!" I say, as Sue uses the phone to ring us both in, "how are you?"

"I'm OK thanks. This is a surprise, you're on time!" she says.

"Makes a change!" I laugh.

The phone rings back twice, which means that we have successfully logged in to the call monitoring system to Social Services.

"Morning Deb, how's Phil?" Sue asks Debbie.

"He's been alright, considering. Do you know, yesterday, the girls were two hours late. I called the office several times and was told by Sarah, that they were just round the corner. It was lies, and I don't like being lied to. I don't like that Sarah." Debbie tells us.

"Two hours? Wow." I say.

"Exactly!" says Debbie, "when the girls got here, I asked them why they were so late, and one of them said it was staffing issues, and the other just burst into tears. I know its not their fault, but the timekeeping is getting ridiculous, and what is this company doing to you lot?"

"We have got some new staff starting next week" Sue says, "so hopefully things will get better from then."

"I hope so, too!" Debbie says, "you girls are all so stressed out and rushed, it can't be good for you or the clients, and crying, that girl was yesterday, because of it all!"

"Oh dear," I say, "right, let's go and get Phil sorted, shall we?"

"You carry on", says Debbie, "I'll do you both a coffee."

"Thanks, Deb" says Sue.

We go into Phil, all smiles, chatting away about his grandchildren who are visiting him later, and discussing television shows whilst

we get him up, showered, dried, creamed and dressed, then help him into his armchair in the lounge.
Debbie brings in Phil's breakfast and our coffees.
I scribble out the care notes while Sue chats to Phil and Debbie.
We drink our coffees, say our goodbyes, phone out, and head off in different directions within 37 minutes.

I arrive at my next call bang on time. My client is a lady with dementia, and whilst she does not know what time of day it is, I still like to arrive on time to make sure she gets her breakfast, as she can become quite agitated when she hasn't eaten and there has been a long gap between her medication times. She does not know who I am, but she has started to associate my motorcycle parked outside the window with someone coming to visit her.
Sometimes she believes I am her childhood friend, sometimes a shop assistant,
sometimes a nurse, sometimes just a visitor. She waves out of the window to me as I take my helmet off, then rushes to the front door.
"Thank God you're here", Betty exclaims, throwing her arms around me, "I've been all alone, its so lovely to see you!"
"Hey Betty!" I say, smiling, "how are you?"
"Come on in!" she says, and I follow her inside. I make her breakfast and give her her tablets. I make her a cup of tea and we sit down and have a chat.

Betty has a half hour call, but she tends to get quite agitated after fifteen minutes and can become aggressive, so her call length is determined by how her mood is.
Today I stay 25 minutes, and use the 5 minutes as travel time to my next call.

My next call has canceled last minute, so I use my now free fifteen minutes to have a rare coffee break and smoke a cigarette. Then I smoke another. I may not get another opportunity.

I do two more half hour calls, getting breakfasts, helping them get washed and dressed, change pads, washing up and feeding pets, then go to meet Sue back at our double up with Gladys.
We've made it for 11.45. Not bad.
I help Gladys to the toilet while Sue heats a microwave meal for her and does the washing up.
Whilst Gladys is in the toilet, Sue and I compare our rotas, and we decide to swap some of our client calls, as Sarah has done the rotas and if we follow them, we will be going back and forth, wasting precious time and petrol.
Nobody in the office gives a shit what we do as long as the calls get covered and they don't have to deal with anything. They're much too busy still begging carers to come in on their days off with false promises of extra days off and shift swaps.

On weekends, like this one, its the person on call who has to deal with it, which happens to be Sue.
Sue's phone rings and she answers, then discusses with another staff member them working a shift tonight as someone's phoned in sick.
They agree to doing six calls, but Sue still needs another seven covering, and we are both too busy with our own impossible rotas with back to back calls.
Sue phones some other staff while I sort Gladys out.
I'm starting to feel tired now, and knowing that I still have another eleven hours to go feels daunting.

My next call is a 20 minute drive away. I get there, microwave a ready meal for an elderly gentleman, make him a cup of tea, serve, and leave in 17 minutes, not staying the full half hour as I am already half an hour late and have another 20 minute drive to my next call.

I heat a ready meal for a lady, fill up her bird feeders in the garden (off the record, as its not in the care plan to do this, but if I don't, I know that she will try to do it herself, and as I have previously found her lying in the garden after having a fall and had to call an ambulance, I feel that it is the safer option to just do it) chat briefly while I scribble care notes, and leave in 20 minutes.

I heat another ready meal for another lady, make a coffee, leave a glass of water by her chair, wash up and leave in 20 minutes.

I spend 15 minutes trying to convince Betty to come inside and stop yelling at the neighbours over the road about a lawnmower that they apparently borrowed and broke (the neighbours inform me that this happened 10 years ago and that they had paid for it to be fixed, but Betty isn't having any of it. She's stuck in a cycle).
I make Betty a sandwich, give her her meds, and manage to calm her down over a cuppa.
I leave in 35 minutes and head home.

I spend 20 minutes at home, having a coffee, refilling my flask, a brief chat with Pete about the rushing around and feeling tired, a quick toilet visit, scoff a piece of toast, smoke two cigarettes, and head back out for round 2.

Sue and I have both arrived early. I jump in her car for five where we smoke a cigarette each and discuss our respective shifts.
"It's so, so shit!" Sue exclaims, "I'm fed up with it! Sarah just dumps all of the work on me now. She messes up the rotas, and then I have to sort it all out. She puts people on rota for a shift on their days off, without asking them, or on their holiday, that she herself has fucking approved, and I have to sort it out. Then she won't answer her fucking phone! Aargggh! Bitch!"
"That does sound shit, Sue," I say, nodding, flicking ash out of the car window and

exhaling smoke, "have you got Betty on your rota later?"

"Yeah I have, why?" she asks.

"She's probably calmed down now, but she was very agitated earlier, and was outside shouting at the neighbours again this afternoon", I tell her, "she calmed down a little after she had had her meds, but I'm thinking that maybe they need to have a look at her medication?"

"OK", says Sue, "I'll let them know in the office on Monday. I've been saying for a while that Social Services need to review her care package, but as usual, nobody gives a shit. I'll have to speak to them myself."

"Thanks", I say, putting my cigarette out. "I've gotta go everything my fucking self in that office, it's so, so shit!" Sue says, throwing her cigarette out of the window.

We go into the call, where we move an elderly and bed-bound gentleman, Charles, up the bed using a slide sheet, empty his catheter bag, and reposition him to make him more comfortable.

This is a half hour call, but as we haven't had to do a pad change, we're out of there in 18 minutes, ready for our 15 minute drive to Gladys.

Sue takes Gladys to the bathroom while I make her a sandwich for her tea, a cuppa and put a yogurt on her plate for a pudding, then fill in the care notes.

I help Sue make Gladys comfortable in the lounge, and we leave in 20 minutes.

I head up to Bishops Wood, a 20 minutes drive away, and complete two calls. One is to give a tablet, heat a ready meal, a nice easy in and out in 15 minutes, then to a lady where Social Services have given only 15 minutes to help a lady get undressed, into her nightclothes, and then make her something to eat. This call always takes at least 20 minutes, sometimes 30, depending on how well she is feeling on any given day.

Back to Penkridge - another 20 minutes drive, and 20 minutes running late.
I do six single calls, making sandwiches, salads and ready meals, six cups of tea, four medications, putting two to bed, then off to meet Sue to put Gladys to bed.
Then a 15 minute drive to Brewood for our last double up with Charles.

Charles has had a loose bowel movement, so we roll him onto his side, clean off as much as we can with toilet paper, then use wet wipes, then warm soapy water and flannels.
Once he's clean and dry, we apply barrier cream to his bottom to reduce the risk of pressure sores, put a clean pad on, fresh pajamas, empty his catheter bag into the night bag (firstly, if there's not much in the day bag, we don't empty it, as opening and closing the tap too often increases the risk of infections, and secondly, we can check that the urine is flowing freely down the tube into the bag and that there are no leaks), slide him

up the bed, reposition him, pour him some fresh juice, and then leave.
Sue and I both drive to Wolverhampton, turning off at different exits on the roundabout.

My last call is an hour long visit, out in the countryside on a farm.
This call is fairly easy - help Doris to undress, get into her nightie, a pad change, cup of Horlicks, and either chat for half an hour, or put her to bed depending on whether she feels ready to go to bed or not.
Most of my colleagues dread coming to Doris. One, because she's situated on a farm in the middle of nowhere, not signposted, and the satnav doesn't take you right to it, and the farm is down a pitch black pot-holed country lane, so if you don't know where you're going and you can't get anyone on the phone to give you directions, you're in for a nice half hour of going back and forth getting lost.
Secondly, because Doris likes to go at her own pace and will not be rushed. And her pace is very, very slow, even at talking.
Thirdly, even if you do manage to finish all the tasks of the call before the hour is up, Doris will keep you there for the full hour, so you can't get off early and more often than not, you end up running over the allocated time.
I like going to Doris. I'm quite patient and take my time with her, chatting away while getting her ready for bed.
I bring her her Horlicks drink and chocolate biscuits, and sit with her in the lounge by the big cosy fire, having a good chat in her

wonderful big old farmhouse, with all of its interesting quirks and original features.
She doesn't want to go to bed yet, so I stay with her, drinking my coffee from my flask and chat with her about flowers that attract bees.
I stay the full hour, then head off, having to pull over on the way home.

I feel so tired. I am only six miles from home, but I have a five minute break from riding, and finish off my coffee with a cigarette, and text Pete to tell him I'm on my way back.
It starts to rain, so I have a jump on the spot to try and wake myself up a bit, and head back.

I get home at 11.25pm, soaked by the rain, pissed off that my waterproofs aren't as waterproof as I had hoped (it says 100% waterproof on the label. It's lies, I tell you! Lies!), tired after working 17 hours on just 5 hours sleep and a piece of toast, hungry, freezing cold, dehydrated, and so I park up, lock my bike, and head inside.

Pete tells me that he's ordered takeout which should arrive soon, and tells me to have a hot shower, and then we'll watch a film in bed with our food.
I kiss him, nod, have a cigarette, then jump in the shower.
I hear the door go, which must be food, followed by the clinking of plates.
I'm so tired I could almost fall asleep stood up in the shower.

I hurry up rinsing off, then dry off, get into my pajamas, then grab my plate of delicious Chinese curry, satay skewers, spring rolls, chips and friend rice, and join Pete in the bed.
I'm so hungry that I wolf down the lot within ten minutes and fall asleep before I know what film we're watching.

Two

My alarm shrieks its unwelcome voice at 5am. I can barely bring myself to get up, as I am so sleep deprived, its unreal.
Two days in a row I have 16-17 hour shifts on 5 hours of sleep, and I have another ahead of me today, followed by an early shift tomorrow. I reluctantly fling the duvet off of me and sit up.
I stand and immediately feel nauseous and dizzy, so ii sit back down for a while as Pete gets up and puts the kettle on for my coffee.
My chest feels tight, my breathing feels a little shallow, and my throat feels raw.
Great. I am ill. Must have been getting caught in the rain last night.
Damn it.
I go to the bathroom, do all of the stuff I need to do in there, and head outside to warm my bike up, drink my coffee and have a cigarette. Smoking is not a great idea when you have a bad chest, but my nicotine addiction is stronger than my health concerns right now, so fuck it.
Pete steps outside and says, "you look awful, honey, maybe you should call in sick."

"Do you know, I think it was getting caught in that heavy rain last night that's done it", I say, finishing my coffee.
"Phone in sick,Rose, you're   exhausted and ill".
"Pete, if I phone in sick, there is literally no staff as it is - there will be nobody to cover my client calls, and all the poor fuckers on shift will have to pick up even more calls on their already impossible rotas! Its not fair to them, or the clients already getting a shit service", I argue.
"If you go to work, you will make yourself worse!" he pleads, "and it isn't your fault that the company don't employ enough staff.
They should use agency of bank staff for this sort of thing!"
I laugh, and say, "our bank staff are all pretty much full time. I'm not   joking!"
"It is your manager's responsibility to cover your shift if you're ill, Rose, and your contract is zero hours. You can turn down work if you can't do it, just like they can chop and change your hours with no notice. It works both ways!" Pete says, arms now folded.
I turn to him, and say, "Look, I'm going in. If I feel really shit, I'll come home, OK?"
"I'm still not happy, but OK", he says, sighing, "you know I'm only trying to help and look after you, don't you?"
"I know", I say, putting my cigarette out, "I love you".
"I love you too", he says, hugging me tightly.

My work phone makes its clunking noise signaling a rota update.

I look at it as I put my helmet on.
Looks like I'm starting in Brewood instead of Wheaton Aston.
For fuck's sake.
It really annoys me when they do this.
I am literally about to leave. If I had left one minute earlier, I would have rode out to Wheaton Aston and had to go back a good 20 minutes drive to where I'm starting now.
It also means that Sarah is sat at her computer at 5.30am switching client calls around giving no notice to carers or clients.
I wave to Pete as I ride off onto the cold, frosty, wintry road, tired, freezing and feeling shit.

I arrive 10 minutes early to my first client, park up, smoke a cigarette and have a sip of coffee.
I feel awful, but I am determined to plod on and get these calls done as soon as possible.
My client, Vicky, puts her cigarette out as I knock and walk in to her cosy lounge.
We chat as I get her washed and dressed, put her cream on her legs, and make her breakfast.
She tells me that she has been unwell the last few days, but is feeling better today. I tell her that I'm feeling a little rough but will be fine once I've had a good night's sleep.
"I'm not surprised", Vicky says, "you lot are all so busy, all of you have bags under your eyes, I can tell none of you get any sleep! What time do you finish today?"
"About 10.30 tonight" I tell her as I scribble some care notes.

"That's a long day", she says, "its not even half six!"

"I know, but there's no rest for the wicked!" I say, smiling.

"I couldn't do your job", she says, "it must be hard, having to look after people all day, and not having time to look after yourself. My granddaughter does care work in a home, and she's tired all the time. I'm grateful for you lot coming to help me, you're all so lovely, but it must be tough".

"It can be", I tell her, "but it makes it easier having lovely clients like you!"

Vicky laughs and says, "I bet you say that to everyone!"

I smile and close the care folder.

I say goodbye and leave 5 minutes early.

I swing round to my next client, whose wife lets me in and tries to give me chocolate.

I politely tell her that it is a bit too early for me to have chocolate, but she insists I put one in my bag for later, so I do, then help her husband get showered and dressed, empty his catheter, and change the bag.

I always check the catheter bags, as they are supposed to be changed at least once weekly, and the date written on it is two weeks ago. His urine is cloudy and his wife tells me that he has been feeling unwell and been a little aggressive over the last few days.

I suggest to her to call the doctor tomorrow, as his urine is cloudy and he may have a urinary tract infection.

I know that we are all rushed off of our feet, but I pride myself on doing my job properly.

Once my client is dressed and seated in the lounge, I flick through the care notes, and see that all of the eight other care workers who attended him over the last seven days did not pick up on the fact that his bag needed changing.

I write that I have changed his bag, and have dated and initialed it.

This is one of the reasons that I get annoyed with having constant rota changes - there is next to no continuation of care for clients. If the same carers went to the same clients most of the time, they would know that catheter bags need changing, and they would notice behavioral changes, they would pick up on things because they were there most of the time.

I do ten more morning calls, getting ten people washed and dressed, make ten breakfasts, make ten beds, administer nine sets of medication, feed six pets, wash up five times, put three loads of laundry on, and go to the shop for bread and milk twice.
This takes me up to 12.45pm.

I do three lunch calls, make three cups of tea, administer two sets of medication, make two ready meals and one sandwich, do one load of laundry, and then get a break at 2.30pm.

I have an hour and a half before shift two, and its not worth going all of the way home to come all the way back.

I give Sue a call and we agree to meet at the trucker's cafe for lunch.

I arrive first and order a coffee, a chicken curry pie with chips and peas, and wait for Sue at a table by the window.
I like it here at the trucker's cafe. It is busy, but all of the clientele consisting of HGV drivers and workmen keep themselves to themselves, having their meals, reading the paper or watching the news on the televisions, or chatting amongst themselves.
Nobody bothers you here.

Sue arrives, orders an all day breakfast with a coffee, yawns and sits down with me.
"Hello Sue, how you doing?" I ask her, sipping my coffee.
"Oh God, I'm so fucking tired! Sarah's still not answering her phone but I know she's working because the rotas keep updating with stupid fucking calls all over the place, and I've got carers ringing me up pissed off that their shifts are changed, so I'm having to get the laptop out to change them around, between doing my own calls, I've been running half an hour late all day, my phone constantly ringing, and I just want to go fucking home!"
She puts her head in her hands.
"Sounds shit", I say, "well, my rota changed as I was leaving the house at half five this morning, so its a good job I noticed before I left else I'd have been running late. I'm only on time because I've cut all my calls down by five or ten minutes".
"Rose, I don't know what to do. Its getting beyond a joke. Have you looked at your rota

for next week?" Sue asks me, drinking her coffee.

"Not yet", I reply, and get my work phone out to have a look.

"You've got to be kidding me", I say, looking at my updated rota for tomorrow, with 27 client visits, all back to back with no travel time, some calls 10 miles away from each other.

"Yep", Sue says, "she puts me in charge of the rotas, so I do them, giving travel time, then she overrides me slotting in calls where there should be breaks and travel time, and doesn't answer her phone when I've got angry carers ringing me up giving me all the shit. Fuck sake!"

Our food arrives and we both tuck in.

"These rotas are impossible!" I say, checking the rest of the following week.

"Yep. When I get home later, I'm gonna sort them all out. You've got carers based in Coven going up to Bishops Wood, and carers based in Bishops Wood going down to Coven. It's stupid! She doesn't care, she just slots them in without thinking. Then you've got Penkridge based carers going to Wolverhampton mid shift, to go all the way back to Penkridge, when there's carers actually in Wolverhampton with an hour's gap in their rota. What the fuck?" Sue complains between mouthfuls.

I nod in agreement, feeling sorry for Sue having to sort out all of this crap.

"How's Wayne these days?" I ask.

Wayne is Sue's partner. They've been having problems lately because Sue is constantly at work, even when she's not supposed to be, and still fixing rotas when she's at home. They never spend time together anymore, and so they've been arguing.

In fact, I think that all of my colleagues are having family and relationship problems, because of the constant work pressures. We're all so exhausted that when we do get a day off, we spend it catching up on sleep and trying to ignore all of the phone calls from work.

"Wayne's pissed off. He says I'm never there, even when I'm physically at home. We haven't had sex in three months. I'm so tired all of the time. And then I saw some texts from his ex on his phone", she says, "I'm worried that he's getting so fed up of me always being at work that he's looking elsewhere".

"Shit, I hope not!" I say, taking another mouthful.

"Well if he is, I don't blame him, to be honest. He's right, I'm never there, we don't have sex anymore, we don't talk. All we talk about is work, and how we never do anything together anymore. What can I do?" she says, clearly upset.

"You can leave this job", I say, "sometimes sanity is better than money".

"I know", she says, sighing, "but I've got bills coming out of my ears. I don't have time to apply for other jobs, or the fucking energy. This is the first thing I've eaten in three days. I literally go to work, go home, and sleep. I have no life."

"Pete and I have been arguing, too. He wanted me to call in sick today because I felt really ill this morning, but I didn't. Obviously I

didn't", I laugh, "because here I am! Day three of sixteen hour shifts and no sleep! Who needs sleep? Or sanity? Or a sex life?"
We both giggle.
"I need sleep and sanity", Sue says.
"I need a sex life!" I say, making her laugh again.
"When did you last have sex?" she asks.
"Erm, last week, I think. On my day off on Tuesday. I slept for thirteen hours, woke up and got a little frisky. I want it at least three times a week, though. This job is getting in the way of that. It's effectively cock blocking me. Think I need to look for something else".
Sue chuckles, and says, "Rose, you're funny, you are".
"Mate, if I can have a steady income, reasonable hours and a bit of sex three times a week, I'm a happy girl. But I'm not getting that, am I? My income is shit, I'm working 70 hours or more a week and getting paid for about 35,because of this travel time issue. What the fuck?"
"It's fucking shit, ay it? I'm doing over 100 hours a week, getting paid for like, 50. They haven't upped my pay yet, either" sue tells me.
"What, you've had a promotion with no pay rise?" I ask, surprised.
"Yep, Sarah said I have to prove I can do the job before I get the pay rise".
"Fuck, Sue! You've got all this responsibility, and no perks! I'd tell them to fuck off! That's why I won't be a senior. I don't want the drama for the sake of an extra twenty pence an hour. So how long is it before you've

proved you can do the job? I mean, you're basically doing the job of two people right now!"

"Sarah said three months".

I almost choke on my last bite of curry pie. Sue sighs, and sips coffee.

We both have a cigarette in the car park before we head off back to work.

"Where are you now?" I ask her.

"Going to Wolverhampton. Where are you?"

"Six calls in Wheaton Aston, then seven in Coven", I tell her.

"Right then", she says, stamping out her cigarette, "I'll see you when I see you. Have a good shift!"

"Ta ra a bit!" I say, putting my helmet on.

We go our separate ways.

I arrive in Wheaton Aston fifteen minutes early, and decide to swap my calls around a bit to make my route better, so I am not going back and forth on myself.

I start early, at 3.45pm, make a sandwich, cup of tea and give medication, and leave ten minutes early at 4.05pm.

The next five clients, which should take three hours including time spent traveling, I mange to get through in two hours and 20 minutes, making five meals, four cups of tea and one coffee, four sets of medication, three loads of laundry and one in the dryer, feed two pets, chatter away about the weather, the news, their families, and I smile away, being friendly and pretending I'm OK when my throat feels

like its on fire, my head feels like its in a vice,
I'm hot and cold, tired and want to go home.
I head to Coven and arrive at my first call at
6.45pm, just on time.
I get through the next six calls - all within 3-5
minutes of each other, which should take me
a total of three hours fifteen minutes - in two
and a half hours, taking me to 9.15pm.

I get to my last call at 9.20pm, a lovely lady
called Maggie, where she likes a cup of cocoa
made for her, a ten minute chat, a seat on the
commode, and then put to bed.
I like Maggie. She is one of those people who
just make you feel warm inside, because she's
so cheery and laid back, and she is like a sort
of favorite Grandma that you would have.
She won't have a cuppa unless you join her,
and she won't let you leave until you do.
I let myself in with the key from the key safe,
and put my helmet, bag and jacket down in
the hallway.
I shout hello, then use the phone to log in
with the call monitoring.
I head into the back room where she is always
sat knitting something for someone's baby -
the next door neighbours', the great-
grandchildren, the local shop keepers' neice -
with the news on the radio in the background.
I look to the chair by the fire where she
always sits, and it is empty.
Her walking frame isn't there either, so
perhaps she's gone to the kitchen.
"Maggie? It's Rose, are you there?" I shout
out, looking around, heading to the kitchen.
No answer.

She can be hard of hearing, so I check around the ground floor.
She's not in the dining room, nor the lounge.
"Maggie, where are you, my love?" I shout louder, starting to worry.
I check the conservatory, the downstairs toilet, the utility room.
All are empty.
She wouldn't have gone out and left the lights and the radio on.
Her walking frame is by the stairwell.
I dash upstairs, calling out, feeling panicky.
No sign of her in the three bedrooms.
I head into the bathroom, and there she is.
And oh, the blood.
Maggie is on the floor, face down, blood all in her blue rinse perm and over the bath.
It looks like she's hit her head.
"Maggie, can you hear me?" I shout, checking for a pulse, and put my head next to hers to listen for breathing.
She is breathing, but very quietly, in short breaths, and her pulse seems low.
At least she is alive.
I grab my phone out of my pocket and dial 999.
I try to remain calm, and explain to the operator the situation quickly and clearly, giving as much information as I can, explaining how to find the house set back from the road, that my black motorcycle is parked outside to help them identify it.
After they've hung up, I fetch a blanket and cover her with it.
I talk to her, reassure her that help is on its way.

I call Sue, who answers the on-call phone, and report the situation to her, and tell her that an ambulance is coming.
She tells me to call her back afterwards and let her know what happens.
I go downstairs and open the front door, ready for the ambulance crew, then go back up to Maggie.
I continue to talk to her, and reassure her that I'm with her.
The ambulance crew arrive, and I shout to them that we're upstairs.
The two paramedics quickly assess Maggie, check for breaks, and get her strapped up to a stretcher.
They ask me if she's ever had a stroke, heart condition, medical conditions, and I show them the care plan, give lists of her medications and give them her next of kin's contact details.
They take her away in the ambulance, and I ring out on the phone, quickly locking up, just desperate to get out of there.
I call Sue back.
"Sue? They've took Maggie in an ambulance and are taking her to hospital. Can you call her granddaughter, Liz, and let her know please?"
"Yep, no worries. Are you OK?" she asks.
I stand next to my bike and take a deep breath.
"Yeah, I'm just a little upset. That wasn't how I expected to end my shift. I just hope she's OK!" I reply.
"Rose, go home and get some sleep, OK? I'm gonna call Liz now and let her know about

Maggie. I'll see you tomorrow. Let me know when you've got back safe", Sue says.
"OK, goodnight", I say, and hang up.
I feel tense as I put my jacket and helmet on. I start up my bike and head home, having to pull over on the way to have a good cry.
I smoke two cigarettes between sobs and sips of coffee.
I'm so fucking exhausted, I know I need to get home, but I can't drive whilst I'm crying because I can't fucking see and its not safe to drive when you're emotional, and I don't fancy having a crash on the way home to top it all off.
I compose myself and carry on home.

Pete has opened the gate ready for me to ride in and park on the driveway.
I open the front door, de-biker by taking off my gloves, helmet and jacket, then grab a glass of wine, and pop into the garden to have a cigarette.

Pete comes outside.
"Where have you been?" he asks, "I was expecting you back forty five minutes ago! You didn't text to say you were coming back like you usually do."
"Sorry, hon, I've had a really crap shift-"
He cuts me off, and says, "you've always had a crap shift, Rose. You're ill, you're working yourself to the bone for a crappy company who won't thank you for it, and you're never here! You're always either *at* work, on the phone *to* work, or thinking *about* work. When

are you going to change your priorities and think about yourself, for once?"

I look at him with teary eyes. I feel so awful, and I wasn't prepared to come home to a discussion about how my job is slowly sucking the life out of me and how I need to get my shit together.

I know its all true, but right now I'm so exhausted and stressed and upset thinking that one of my favorite clients may well be dying...

I just can't talk to him about it.

My brain just will not allow me to express any kind of comprehensible explanation of what I am feeling.

So I stand in silence with my cigarette and my wine and just cry.

Pete puts his arms around me and holds me while I cry and cry some more.

My hands are shaking with stress and I drop the wine glass - one of my favorites - which makes me cry more as I stare at the smashed glass and watch the red spread out over the paving.

Pete leads me inside, tells me to get in the shower, and goes out to clear up the glass.

I undress and just sit on the floor of the shower cubicle, the hot water cascading down on me, shaking and sobbing.

I feel broken.

Pete comes in once he's finished and looks at me with sad eyes.

"Look at what this job is doing to you! This isn't healthy!" he says, and goes to warm up my dinner.

I get up, wash, dry, put pajamas on, and sit in the bed.
Pete brings me my meal of chicken curry and rice.
I eat it and fall asleep.

My alarm shrieks once more at 5am, and I drag myself out of the covers to turn it off.
This morning, I feel even worse.
My head is pounding with each unusually fast beat of my heart.
My eyes feel dry and hot, and waves of nausea sweep me each time I attempt to stand up.
Oh goodness, I feel shit today.
Lack of sleep is well and truly kicking in.
I mentally tell myself to 'pull it together, Rose!' and force myself to get up.
Pete gets up, makes me coffee, and turns to look at me as I sip my glorious caffeinated beverage with teary and tired eyes.
"You're not going to work today", he informs me.
I sip away, taking in what he has just said.
"Yes, I am going to work" I tell him.
"The state you are in, means that you aren't safe to be driving, let alone giving medication to people! Look at you!" he shouts.
I sip my coffee, and say calmly, "Pete, I am going to go to work. There is no-one to cover my shift. I am going in, and you can't stop me."
"Rose, you are exhausted and ill! You are not fit to go to work! I'm not letting you go!" Pete argues.

I walk away, go outside for my cigarette and start up my bike.

Pete comes outside and switches the engine off.

"You're not going! Just phone in sick!" he shouts.

"What the fuck, Pete! I said I'm going in!" I yell back, starting my bike up again.

"No!" he says, standing in front of the gate.

I finish my cigarette, put my helmet and gloves on, and start walking my bike to the gate.

"Pete, get out of the way!" I yell.

"No!" he shouts back, "you're not well, you need a fucking day off! Phone in sick! You'll end up in an accident, you're not fit to work! Look at how you were last night! You need rest!"

There is desperation in his voice.

I rev my bike up and keep heading towards the gate, feeling pissed off with him.

"Pete, fucking MOVE!" I yell.

My poor neighbours can probably hear us, but I'm stressing that my shift is supposed to start in 25 minutes.

"If you come near this gate, Rose, I will fucking kick your bike over! You are not going!"

"Get out of the way!" I scream at him, moving towards the gate.

He kicks out and I brake.

"WHAT THE FUCK, PETE!"

"ROSE!"

I can't deal with this this morning.

I get off my bike and stand, glaring at him.

"I'm not phoning in sick, Pete!" I tell him.

"Yes you are!" he shouts, "you can't work today!"
I stare at him through angered tears.
"You phone in sick for me, then!" I shout, "I'm not doing it, because I actually want to go to work!"
Pete takes my phone from me and calls the on-call.
Sue answers.
Pete starts telling her that I'm not coming in today because I'm too exhausted and I'm ill.
She asks to speak to me.
By this point I feel furious and so emotional that I can barely speak.
Pete passes me the phone.
"Hi, Sue", I say.
Pete starts shouting in the background, and I can't hear what she's saying.
"Rose, can you go somewhere where your boyfriend isn't shouting in the background, please?" Sue says.
"Hang on", I tell her.
Pete is still shouting.
"Pete, can you go inside, please?" I ask.
"Rose, you're not going in! Don't let them talk you into it! You aren't well!" he shouts.
"Pete, go inside, please!" I shout.
He walks off angrily.
"Hi Sue", I say.
"Are you not working today, then?" she asks.
"Pete was physically stopping me from leaving", I tell her, and start crying again, "Sue, I think he's right. I'm not in a fit state to work today. I'm so fucking tired, and I feel so shit!"

"Rose, I know its shit. Its just that you've called like, twenty minutes before your shift starts. I'm gonna have to drive up there now, there's no-one to cover at such short notice", Sue says.

"I'm sorry, Sue. I had such a shit night last night, and I can't stop fucking crying. I can't go into clients crying my eyes out, can I?"

"No, you can't", she sighs, "OK, well, get some rest, and I'll speak to you soon, OK?"

"OK. Speak soon".

I hang up and head inside.

I'm still crying, but I feel furious.

"How fucking DARE you do that to me?!" I shout.

Pete stands in the kitchen, flabbergasted.

"Rose, look in the mirror! You look terrible! You look half dead!" he responds, sounding hurt, "I care about what happens to you! I'm trying to help you! Its all very well trying to plod on, but you are making yourself ill! You don't know when to stop! You need rest!"

We spend the rest of the morning screaming at each other, both of us trying to get our points across - him wanting me to see how much this job has affected me and wanting me to put myself first, and me wanting him to see that I didn't like him telling me that I couldn't do something - until we both decide we need some space.

Pete packs a few things and goes back to his flat for a couple days.

I'm not sure how I feel about this yet, but I accept that its probably for the best.

I text Sue to tell her that I won't be in tomorrow either, to give her a heads up to arrange cover in advance.
I do need a rest, and I have peace and quiet to be completely alone with my thoughts, now that Pete has gone away for a bit.
I know that he is only concerned about me, but my head is currently such a mess in its sleep deprived state that I can barely make heads or tails out of anything.
I lie in bed for a few hours and sleep.

When I wake up, I wake naturally at 5pm.
I feel like I'm hungover. I probably need a good week of sleep to get over the exhaustion properly. It has been months since I slept well, and actually had enough sleep.

Care work can be such a lonely occupation. You spend all day looking after other people, listening to their problems, trying to make life easier for them, whilst neglecting your own family and friends, slowly isolating yourself from the real world, because you're a shift worker who barely has enough time between shifts to sleep, let alone spend actual quality time relaxing, socialising and winding down. People in the real world eventually give up inviting you to things, because you're always at work, or too tired, or have no money because it goes straight back out on putting fuel in your vehicle's tank so that you can get to work, and you work all the hours you can get so that you can pay your bills, only to be ripped off by the zero hours loop holes, so you end up working and working and working, running yourself further and further down into this deep, deep hole where there is no escape.

At least, that is how it feels.

Right now, when I am alone with my thoughts, I feel as though I want to just give up.

Like I said, welcome to the world of a Domiciliary Care Assistant.

Three

I wake up to no alarm at 10am. I'm feeling rather pleased that I have the flat to myself, and haven't got to go to work today.
I've really needed a little break from all of the stress.
My phone is currently turned off. I think I'll leave it till I've had a coffee before I turn it on. I need to brace myself before I deal with all of the voice mails from colleagues begging me to work and cover calls.
Yep.
I'll give it a while.
I make a coffee and sit outside in my thick winter dressing gown.
The sun is out, making the last of the frost on the paving sparkle.
I watch my breath mist and enjoy the cold fresh air.
It is so quiet.
All I can hear is bird song.
I light a cigarette and drink my warm coffee in the cold morning air, feeling nice and peaceful.

Even my internal dialogue is quiet this morning. Usually, by now, it is a constant chattering in my head, thoughts flying about in there, overpowering and overbearing.
I sit quietly enjoying the silence.

Once the novelty has worn off and I realise how cold I feel, I go inside and turn on my CD player, and blast out a bit of Sheryl Crow.
Angry woman music always makes me feel good in the morning.
Sod the neighbours.
They know where I live should they wish to complain.
I go in the shower and have a wash, noticing how hairy I have become.
I started my job three months ago, and I haven't had the time or the energy to shave my legs since then. I know its winter, but come on! I can't believe how much I've let myself go!
I weigh myself and see that I've put over a stone on in weight. No wonder my trousers are getting so tight!
I study my figure in the mirror.
I am almost horrified.
Three months ago, I was a size 10. I was healthy-looking, and had a glow about me.
My hair was shiny, and my eyes were bright.
I look at my dull, lifeless face.
I have dark circles around my once bright eyes.
My hair is scraggly looking, and the shine gone. In fact, it is thinner since it started falling out last month due to stress.

I am no longer toned. I have no time to work out now. I have become wobbly and flabby.
I start to cry again.
I feel that I have let myself down.

I go to the kitchen and open a bottle of wine.

Fuck it.
I'm not working today.
If I want to get pissed, I bloody well will!
Come on, Sheryl Crow, let's fucking party!

After a good hour or so of dancing around the living room in my nightgown, downing a bottle of red and shouting out the lyrics to two Sheryl Crow albums, I feel that I've got whatever it was out of my system and sit down on the sofa.

What am I doing with my life?

What, am I actually, fucking, doing? Really?

I'm getting pissed on a Tuesday morning (afternoon, now, actually, like that makes it more acceptable...) feeling a bit shitty, and feeling, let's face it, like I am generally failing at life.

I got into care because I wanted to make a difference.
I quit a boring cleaning job that I'd stuck at for three years, because my boss was a complete dick that I'd had enough of for the last three years, and because I wanted to do something more with my life.

I wanted to *feel* like I was doing something more with my life.

Instead?
Well, now I feel like I can't even COPE with life. For fuck's sake!
I have found a job that I have a real passion for, am really good at, but that I can't bloody cope with because of unrealistic workloads and pressures.
Maybe I should look for another job in care.
The other staff have said that all care companies are the same.
That can't be true, can it?
I won't know until I try.

I get the laptop out and apply for ten care work vacancies across the west midlands who are paying more than minimum wage.
I figure that even if I get the same shit elsewhere that I get now, I may as well be paid more for it!
I close the laptop lid, crack open another bottle of red and blast out some more tunes on the stereo.
I WILL be successful and enjoy my job one day.
Bit of James Brown, followed by some 90's dance tunes.
Sorry, neighbours, I'm having a party by my fucking self and you're not invited!

Maybe I'm having a bit of a breakdown.
Maybe I don't fucking care.
Maybe I do care, but maybe I don't want to fucking care so fuck it, fuck you, and fuck off!

Yeah.
Fuck everything.

I continue drinking and decide that I should get dressed and go to the shop to buy some food as there is nothing good in the fridge.
I have opened and closed it several times, thinking that maybe, just maybe, the next time I open it, something good will appear that I didn't notice the previous time I opened it.
This has proved to be a complete waste of time.
I get dressed and stumble up the road to the shop.
I bump into one of my old work colleagues from my previous cleaning job, Julie, as she comes out of the chip shop.
"Hi, Rose!" she exclaims, "how are you?"
Fuck.
I am so not prepared for this kind of social encounter.
Bollocks.
"Oh hi Julie, I'm good thanks, how are you?" I say brightly, trying my best to not seem as pissed as I currently feel.
I am trying to stay still and not sway.
I feel like I'm swaying.
"Really good, thanks. How's your new job?" she asks.
My new job?
It's shit.
I'm pissed on a fucking Tuesday because I hate it so much.
"I love it, Julie, I'm really enjoying it" I lie.

I know she'll go back and tell my old supervisor, Jean, who hates me.
I want that bitch to think I'm having a great fucking time away from her.
"Oh good, I'm really pleased for you. We all miss you, you know!" Julie says.
I hope she doesn't notice how pissed I am.
The fresh air outside has made me feel even more drunk.
"Well, Julie, I've gotta go to the shop and get supplies. Lovely seeing you!" I say quickly.
I hope I didn't slur those words.
"OK, Rose, take care, now!" she says.
I smile and rush off around the corner to safety.
I go to the shop and successfully manage to place items of food into my basket without bumping into the shelves too much, get to the till, purchase more wine, and get it home without too much trouble walking in an almost straight line.
Great stuff.
I put a frozen pizza into the oven, eat some donuts whilst it cooks, and continue my party.
I feel better already!
I brave turning my phone on.
I have a voice mail from Sarah. She says that she's taken my calls off of me for tomorrow morning and tomorrow night just in case I'm not feeling well.
That will be my punishment for having a couple days off.
Another day of no work and no pay.
Well fuck you, Sarah!
I will still be over the drink drive limit in the morning so I wasn't coming to work, anyway!

Ha!
I have a text from Sue asking if I want a shift in Wolverhampton tomorrow night.
Maybe I don't.
Maybe I do. I will be sober by then and at least its money, plus, the shift she's offering is a double up run where I won't have to drive anyway, I'll be able to jump in with whoever I'm on shift with.
I text back and say yes to the night shift.
Sue replies saying OK, and sends the rota through.
Great, I'm working with Gina all night.
I like Gina, and she lives near to me so I'll probably get a lift from her.
I text Gina and ask for a lift.
She agrees.
Great stuff.
Fuck you, Sarah! I'm working tomorrow night just to piss you off!

I eat pizza in bed whilst watching medical dramas on the laptop and decide that I should stop drinking now, have a final cigarette before bed, then fall asleep as soon as my head hits the pillow.

Pete calls me at 11am.
I tell him that I've got work tonight, but feel much better for having time off.
He says that he's glad, and has enjoyed having a bit of peace and quiet to himself.
We agree for him to come and stay over tomorrow night.
I have missed him a little, but I needed to get some things out of my system, I guess.

I make fish fingers for lunch and watch a couple episodes of medical dramas, then get ready for work.

I walk into town to meet Gina.

She arrives 10 minutes late, but assures me it will be fine.

"Rose, I fly through these calls, I'm tellin' ya, this is my regular run. We'll be done by nine", she tells me.

"It says half ten on the rota", I reply.

"Fuck that! Mate, we'll get through them quicker than that!You'll see!"

We start at 4.15pm, 15 minutes late, with a male client.

This is supposed to be a half hour call.

We assist him to the toilet, give him privacy, heat his ready meal while he's in there and make him a cup of coffee, assist him off the toilet, clean him up, back into his armchair to watch the football and serve his meal. A quick chat while Gina writes the care notes, then we're off in 17 minutes.

Next is another male client. His is supposed to be a half hour call, but as his daughter is there making his meal and she tells us that she's just taken him to the toilet, and he says that he doesn't need, so we stay to chat for 10 minutes, scribble in the care plan, and leave, saving 20 minutes.

Off to a female client with a 30 minute call. She requires the use of a hoist to move her from the chair to the bed, which we quickly do.

Gina is so easy to work with, she knows these clients well, their likes and dislikes, and talks me through what to do and when.

We hoist the client onto the bed, a quick pad change and freshen up, hoist her back into her chair, I go downstairs to make her a cup of tea while her son cooks her dinner, and Gina fills out the care notes.

In and out in 20 minutes.

Next is another female client with a 30 minute call. She says that she doesn't need the toilet, just her catheter emptying, which I do while Gina does the washing up. Our client tells us that she's not long eaten and doesn't want anything. We chat for five while I fill out the care notes. Out in 16 minutes.

Another male client with a 30 minute call. We make him a ready meal, cup of tea, hoist him onto the commode, clean him up afterwards, hoist him back onto his chair, clean the commode out, close the curtains, administer his medication, wash up, have a chat, scribble notes, and we're out in 27 minutes.

We go to a male client with a 30 minute call, administer his eye drops, make him 2 cups of tea, a sandwich, hoist him onto his bed so that he can use his urine bottle, empty it once he's done, hoist him back into his wheelchair, chat for a while, feed his dog, and off in 25 minutes.

Back to the first client, where we help him to the toilet again, give him a wash and dry, he does his teeth, then help him into his pajamas, and walk with him back into the lounge. His wife says that she will put him to bed later, and that she's just made him a cup of tea. We're out in 22 minutes.

Next is a female client with a 15 minute call. We make her a sandwich and a cup of tea, give her her medication, chat briefly, and we're out in 10 minutes.

Another female client with a 30 minute call. We hoist her onto the commode, change her pad, clean her up, help her undress and into her nightie, give her her medication and a coffee, hoist her onto her bed, make her comfortable, scribble care notes, and we're gone in 25 minutes.

We go to a male client now, a 30 minute call, but as his wife has already done pretty much everything else, we just help him into his pajamas, put his ear drops in, give him a tablet, and we're off in 10 minutes.

Back to the male client with the dog - another 30 minute call. We let the dog out to do his business, administer the client's eye drops, apply creams, hoist him onto the bed, help him to undress, empty his urine bottle once he's finished, put the dog on the bed, park his electric wheelchair and lock up within 27 minutes.

Last call - a female client. We empty her catheter bag, help her to undress and into her nightie, hoist her onto the bed, attach the night bag to her catheter bag, have a quick tidy up, a quick chat, scribble care notes, and we are done by 8.57pm.

On the way back to the car, I tell Gina how surprised I am that we managed 12 client visits in under 4 hours.

"Rose, whenever I've complained that there's too many on my rota, Sarah always says to cut the calls. So I cut the calls. End of the day, as long as everything the client wants is done, and they're safe, what difference does leaving a few minutes early make? Some of them don't want you hanging around chatting when you've finished." Gina says.

We get in and drive off.

"I agree that not all clients want you to hang about, but some of them do. Some of them don't see anybody all day and want to chat, or they feel rushed when you're trying to get in and out as fast as possible", I say.

"I know, mate, but if we'd stayed the full time tonight, with 12 calls, and travel time, we'd be finishing later, and not getting home till after eleven. We'm being paid shit money for what we do, and end of the day, we aint getting enough sleep as it is, so finishing earlier works out better for us", Gina says, "you've been here a few months now, you know the score. We aint got time to care. We aint got time to sit and chat, its a case of getting what needs to be done, done, and the faster the better. They don't give us time to get between clients, so its either run late, or cut the calls short".

"I know, Gina, but it's not fair on the clients. I mean, how long does it take in the morning for you to get up, go to the toilet, have a shower, get dressed and eat your breakfast?" I ask.

"Mate, it takes me like, at least an hour!" Gina laughs.

"Exactly. Now, imagine you couldn't have an hour. Imagine that you had to get it done in half an hour, and you felt ill, and somebody was there rushing you to get out the shower", I say.

"I'd be pissed off! I'd tell whoever was rushing me to fuck off!"

"That's probably what our clients feel like! That's the point!" I tell her.

"I know", Gina says, "but it is the way it is, we can only do so much. If we'm only being paid for half an hour, that's all they get."

"But they don't even get that, sometimes!" I say.

"I know, it aint fair to them, but Rose, you'm only gonna stress yourself out thinkin' about it like that. If it aint Social Services trying to cut costs and cutting their times down, its this fuckin' company puttin' too many calls on our rotas and forcin' us to cut the calls. They even tell us to cut the calls. They get so much money having all these clients but they aint got enough staff, and can't keep the staff they've got. Nobody wants to work this hard for minimum wage. You can work less hours in a supermarket for more money than you get here!"

"Why aren't we all working in supermarkets, then?" I say, laughing.

"Mate, I don't even fuckin' know anymore!"

Gina drops me off and I go inside, pour a glass of wine, and sit outside smoking while thinking about things.

I check my emails, and see that I've had an interview invitation from another care firm.

I decide that I'll call tomorrow after my early shift.

I will get another job, and get away from this awful company, and earn more money!

I'm not going to tell anyone that I'm thinking of leaving, though, as some of them are gossips.

I'll wait till I've gotten something else, then I'll quietly go.

It's near the end of November now. I hope I get something next month so that I can start the new year with a new job.

I indulge in another glass of wine, jump in the shower, and head to bed.

It feels strange in the bed without Pete. I've been Pete-free for three nights now, and right now I miss him terribly.

I call him so that I can hear his voice.

"Hey honey", I say when he answers the phone, "I just wanted to hear your voice before I go to sleep".

"Aww, bless you, I love you", he says, "I'll be over tomorrow, don't you worry!"

"Pete, I love you. I'm going to bed now, I just wanted to tell you that I love you", I say.

Pete laughs and says, "I love you too, honey. Goodnight, then!"

"Goodnight Pete!" I say, and hang up.

I fall asleep after a while, tossing and turning, going hot and cold.

My alarm shrieks at 5am. The familiar dread fills me.
I head to the kitchen to make my own coffee, and tell myself that today WILL be a good day, today WILL go smoothly, and I WILL enjoy my shift, I will be POSITIVE, and I will kick ass because I am awesome.
I check my rota for updates, chain smoke two cigarettes whilst drinking coffee, fill my flask, set my satnav up for the first call, because I don't know any of the clients on my rota today.

Not a single one.
I don't even know the areas on my rota today.
Today I am based in Codsall. I didn't know we even covered Codsall, but apparently we now do.
I receive a text from Gina, who is pissed off and asks me if I have a random area on my rota as well as she's been placed in Wombourne today.
Sue calls me as I am about to reply to Gina.
"Hi Sue", I say.
"Alright Rose. Thought I'd call before you left for work. Have you seen your updated rota today?" she asks.
"Yeah, since when do we cover Codsall and Wombourne?" I ask.
"We've had areas from other branches dumped on us because they're having staffing issues. Things are gonna get shit for the next couple months", she says solemnly.
"We have staffing issues!" I argue.

"Yes, but apparently our tiny branch has more staff than the others. The director of the company has done this, not Sarah, for once. Just giving you a heads up that the next few weeks will be tough", she says, "good luck today!"

"Thanks, I think!" I laugh, and hang up.

Great.

I'm definitely calling that company about interview today.

I text Gina and tell her that I'm in Codsall today.

She replies that things are getting worse and that she wants to leave.

Join the club.

I head off.

My first call is a 45 minute shower call with a female client, Joyce. I arrive 10 minutes early and let myself in with the key from the key safe.

I place my things in the hall and call out a loud 'hello'.

"Morning!" Joyce calls out from the room ahead of me.

I push the door open and smile.

Joyce is sat by the fire in her dressing gown.

"Morning Joyce, I'm Rose. I've not been to you before. What can I do for you this morning?" I ask.

"Hello Rose, don't worry, I'm sure we'll manage. Have you got time to help me in the shower?" she asks.

"Yes, I have, Joyce. Just tell me where you want me", I tell her.

"Right, that's great. The girls don't usually have time to shower me, so I'm glad!" she says, getting up out of the chair.

The information I've been given says that this is a shower call. 45 minutes tends to be enough time to give clients a quick shower.

I have a quick flick through the care plan to check what this call entails, while Joyce puts her slippers on.

The care plan tells me that the morning shower call is 45 minutes, giving a shower, assisting dressing, applying creams, making breakfast, emptying and cleaning out the commode, making the bed.

I check what the other staff have been writing in the care notes.

Over the last four weeks, most of them have only been there 25-30 minutes, not staying the full time.

They have only been giving her a quick body wash.

I dare say that they have been as rushed as our branch, but still, she hasn't been given a shower in almost a month.

Joyce shows me upstairs, and I collect her clothes from her bedroom.

I assist her in the shower. She does most of her wash herself, I just help washing her back and legs, then help dry her off, apply her creams, and help her to get dressed.

She tells me that the service from the other branch has been awful, and whilst the staff were all lovely, she was always rushed.

We go downstairs, where she tells me that she will make her own breakfast, as she likes to stay independent.

I empty and clean out her commode, make her bed, open all of the curtains, sit down with her in the lounge while she eats her cereal, and I scribble out the care notes.

I leave within 38 minutes.

My satnav takes me to the next address, to a male client. He has a 15 minute call. He is already eating the breakfast he has made for himself, and has a cup of coffee made. He tells me his blood sugar readings, which I jot down in the care notes, and tells me that this is really just a checking in call to make sure he's OK and has everything he needs.

I leave in 10 minutes.

Next call, the satnav doesn't take me to. I spot a Royal Mail van down the muddy country lane I'm on, pull over next to it and ask the postman for directions.

Postal workers are great, they know where everything is because they have to deliver there.

I follow the directions given and find the little farmhouse where my next client, an elderly lady, lives.

I ring the bell, and she answers the door.

"Hello", she says, "are you the carer?"

"Hi Eve, yes, I'm Rose", I say politely with a smile.

"Well, Rose, you can go if you like, because I've already done it all. I'm so used to nobody coming till the afternoon that I got fed up with it and just started doing it all myself. It hurts me, but I've had to manage", Eve tells me.

"I'm sorry to hear that, Eve! Is there anything I can do, seeing as I'm here now?" I ask.

"No, love, I'm fine. I'm surprised somebody's turned up on time, to be honest! You get off, I know how busy you all are!"

"Are you sure?" I ask.

"I'm sure, see you again", she says, and closes the door.

I head back to my bike, select the option 'client declined' on my work phone app, and head off early to my next call.

Next is another shower call with a female client named Jean. Her daughter answers the door to me, and shows me through to the back room where Jean is sat.

"Hi Jean, I'm Rose. How are you?" I ask, smiling.

"Hello love, I'm alright thank you. You don't need to do anything, my daughter, Rita, has done everything. She's had me in the shower and sorted my breakfast", Jean says.

I look to Rita.

"Your company's service has been horrendous!", Rita tells me, "sometimes Mom's had to wait until one o'clock for her breakfast, for someone to come, and by that time she's wet the bed, she can't get out of it herself. It's not good enough! I work part time, so on the mornings I have off work, I've been having to come over to look after her and do what your company should be doing!"

"My goodness, I'm sorry to hear that!" I say, shocked the more I hear, "what can I do now that I'm here?" I ask.

"Nothing", Rita says, "I've done everything, like I said. I know its not your fault - you've come on time - we're just that used to an appalling service, it's been easier to just do it. Mom can't wait till one o'clock to get out of bed, to have breakfast!"

"I'm from another branch, so this area is new to me. Has the service from the other branch always been this bad?" I ask Jean.

"Pretty much", Jean says, "the last few months have been the worst, with all the girls leaving, and these new ones who start, well, they haven't got a clue what they're doing. It gets frustrating having to explain to them what to do, especially when it's someone different every day. Its never the same carer who comes. But the timekeeping is the worst bit".

Rita nods, and says, "we're looking at other companies, to be honest. Your firm was the only one who could fit Mom in at the time, but we're trying to move now. We've had enough. Mom's been so ill with upset over it!"

"I'm so sorry that its been like that for you!" I say to them.

"Do you want your book to fill in?" Rita asks, passing me the care plan folder.

"Yes, thank you", I say, taking it.

I write that Jean's daughter was here and had tended to all of Jean's needs, that Jean has been unhappy with the services, and that no care was required at this time.

I leave in 7 minutes.

Wow.

Two calls where the clients have had to manage.
The more I hear, the more angry I feel about how this company is letting down the people who they are supposed to be caring for.
A care company that doesn't care.

I am now running 50 minutes early, so I ride half a mile up the road, pull over, light a ciggie, pour some coffee, and phone the other care company about getting an interview.
I book an interview for Friday next week, on my day off.
I feel good, thinking about how I may be able to escape from this awful company.
I care about these clients, but I can't keep running myself into the ground like this.

I arrive 20 minutes early to my next call, a lady who has poor mobility.
This is a single call, and supposed to be 30 minutes.
She is unable to stand up on the stand aid. She hasn't the energy or the strength to weight bear on her legs.
She needs a pad change, as I can smell her faeces and her pajama bottoms are wet and stained.
I call the office and speak to the branch manager, Sarah.
"Hi Sarah, I'm with Mrs Jones, and she's unable to weight bear. She can't stand, and she's in a bit of a mess. I can't help her onto the commode by myself. What do you want me to do?" I ask her.

"Oh God, erm, I'm thinking... can you leave Mrs Jones and go to Mr Leighton next?" Sarah says.

"Sarah, Mrs Jones has faeces leaking from her pad, she needs to get cleaned up and I don't feel comfortable leaving her like this. Can you send another carer to me to help, please?" I reply.

"Rose, there isn't anyone else working on the Codsall run this morning. If you go to Mr Leighton and get his call out the way I can try and get someone off the Penkridge run to come to you", she says, "but it probably won't be till half one, if they can get down to you".

"It's half eight, I can't leave her like this for five hours!"

"Can you not just get her on the commode? She's only small, just help her stand up. Do what you can", Sarah says.

I'm starting to get pissed off.

"Sarah, is there not someone on the Coven run you can send to me? Coven is nearer to me, and I'm not comfortable moving her on her own. This is a two person job if I'm to do it safely!"

I'm trying my best to stay calm, feeling angrier by the second.

"Just do what you can, Rose, I've got to go, OK? Bye", she says, hanging up.

I could scream.

I don't scream, however.

I go back in to my client, smile, and say, "OK, I'm gonna do my best for you. Let's try again, shall we?"

I support Mrs Jones from the back, turn the stand aid and pull the commode right behind her.

I hold her up with one arm at the back of her, use the other to pull her trousers down as quickly as possible and take the soiled pad out, placing it in one of those dog mess bags, and lower her down onto the commode.

That proved to be very difficult.

I'm not insured to do this, and I'm not comfortable doing this by myself. Quite frankly, it puts both me and the client at risk, but I cannot leave someone lying in their own shit for five hours on the off chance that my manager will 'try' to send someone down here to help,'if they can get down' to me, meaning that in reality, I'm on my own, here.

I grab a bowl of warm soapy water, and wash down Mrs Jones while she sits on the commode, dry her off, dress her top half, help her up, support her again with one arm while cleaning her bottom with a flannel in the other, dry her off, grab the clean pad, put it in place, pull up her knickers and clean trousers, spin the stand aid around, and help her into the armchair.

I then empty the commode upstairs, clean it out, bring it back down, put it away, move the stand aid out, throw the rubbish out in the outside bin, empty the bowl of water, throw the flannels and towel into the washing machine, put the full load of washing on, tidy up, ask Mrs Jones what she wants for breakfast, go and make her the toast with marmalade and a coffee, bring it to her, give her her medication, open the curtains, then hurriedly write the care notes as I've been here for over an hour and am now running late, say my goodbyes, and head over to Mr Leighton's.

Mr Leighton's son answers the door and informs me that they are just on their way out to go shopping, and tells me that they had canceled his morning call yesterday.
I head back to my bike and select the 'late cancellation' option on my phone's app.

I do three more calls, washing and dressing clients, make three breakfasts, four cups of tea, two loads of laundry, feed one pet, write one shopping list, empty two commodes, make three beds, find a channel on one television, and then have a 10 minute break at 12.15pm.

I've had a missed call from the office, so I call back, and speak to Sarah.
"Oh, it was just a quickie to say that I can't get anyone to come down to you, so you'll have to manage, I'm sorry!" Sarah says.
"I've sorted it, I did it by myself in the end", I tell her, feeling angry.
"Oh good, see? I knew you'd be alright!" she says brightly.
Fuck you, Sarah.
"Also, Mr Leighton's son said he canceled his call yesterday, they were going out as I arrived", I tell her.
"Oh, did they? No worries. Any chance you can do me a favor and do a call in Coven for

me later? Mrs Brewer? Quick fifteen minute lunch call?" she asks.
"Yep, I should be done here by one, just one lunch call so I'll head over afterwards", I say.
"Thanks babe!" she says and hangs up.
I sip my coffee, have another cigarette to try and calm down, then head to my final call in Codsall.

Back to the gentleman from this morning, with another 15 minute call. He is sat eating his ready meal on arrival, and tells me that there is nothing to do. We chat for five while I scribble care notes, then I head over to Coven.

I arrive at Mrs Brewer's at 1pm, go in, warm her up some soup, serve with bread, a yogurt and a banana, chat for five, write my notes and I'm out at 1.12pm.

Standing by my bike, I call Sue.
"Hey Sue, who's working in Coven today?" I ask her.
"Lisa and Beck, I think, why?" she asks.
"I've finished now and I've just done a call there. I'll ring them and see if they need a hand", I tell her.
"I know Beck's struggling, she's running an hour late, she just rang me to see if I could help but I'm in Wednesfield", she says.
"OK, I'll call Beck. How are you getting on?"
"Well, not too bad, only 20 minutes late but I'll catch up. How have you managed to finish so early?" she says.

"Two clients had already done everything as they were sick of waiting, and one canceled", I reply.
"Lucky you", she says, "I'll speak to you later. Bye!"

I give Beck a call.
"Hey Beck, I'm in Coven, do you want a hand?" I ask.
"Rose you'm a legend! I'm like, an hour late! Can you do Mr Richards and Mrs Phillips? I'm still doing morning calls!"
"Yeah, are they lunch calls?" I ask.
"Yeah they am. My God, how crazy has it gone today?"
"I was on the Codsall run and mine was fairly easy, had three cancellations, but one call where it should have been a double up, really. Client couldn't stand and I was there over an hour!" I tell her.
"Oh God, didn't Sarah send someone to help ya?" she asks.
"Did she fuck! Right, speak later, I'll go to Mr Richards now. See ya!"
"Ta ra, Rose!" she says and hangs up.

Mr Richards and Mrs Phillips are only a few streets away from each other, and both are fairly easy 30 minute calls, but I manage to do the two calls in 50 minutes, and now Beck will be running on time.

I get home at 2.45 to a shocked Pete.
"Wow, you're early!" he says, coming out to me and giving me a kiss and a big cuddle.

"Yeah, I'm actually late, was supposed to finish at half one, but I had cancellations, so I picked up three calls in Coven to help out the others", I tell him, enjoying breathing in his scent.
I have missed him.
"You normally aren't back till half three, even when you finish at twelve!" he says, locking my bike up for me.
"I know, nice to be early!" I say, drinking the remainder of my coffee from my flask, and lighting a cigarette.

Pete buys us a pizza for our lunch/dinner, and we share a bottle of wine, watching a comedy film in bed.
I have turned my phone off, as I've had missed calls from work and I know it will only be the office wanting me to work tonight.
I've decided that I won't be bullied into taking extra shifts anymore. Overworking myself is no good for me, and I'm enjoying just chilling out with Pete so much. We never get the chance to anymore, because I'm always too knackered to do anything, or busy at work.
Enough's enough.
I tell Pete about my interview next week and he's delighted for me.
It is time for things to change.

Four

As I arrive early for Gladys on my usual rota and wait for my double up partner to arrive, I hear my work phone making its clunking noise several times.

Great.

I look at it, and see that I have extra calls slotted in on where my 20 minute break should have been, where my 30 minute travel time should have been to Bishops Wood and back, and another two calls added onto the end of my rota in Wolverhampton.

I feel so fed up of this.

I call the On Call phone.

"Hi Rose", Sarah answers.

"Hi Sarah, my rota has just changed, and you've taken away my travel time to Bishops Wood and back by adding extra calls. That means I'll be running really late", I tell her, "Can you take them out please?"

"I can't, babe, I've got three staff off sick", she says.

"OK, I'll just have to run late then. The two in Wolverhampton at the end, though, I can't do. I need to be home by two", I tell her.

"I really need you to do them, there isn't anyone else to do them!" she says, "I'm desperate to get these calls covered!"

Normally I would have said yes.

Normally I would have felt some kind of guilt.

Normally I would crumble.

Today I am determined not to.

"No, Sarah, I have a doctors appointment today, I'm not doing those calls. Goodbye!" I say, and hang up.

Fuck off, Sarah.

Rose aint taking no more of your shit, mother fucker!

I feel good, now.

I sip some of my coffee, waiting for my partner, Constance, who is now five minutes late.

Constance is usually pretty good with her timekeeping, and is really easy to work with. She's been working in care for years, mainly in care homes, and says that she preferred working in a home, as Dom care is a joke with its awful pay and mileage allowance.

I decide to give it 10 minutes before I call her.

Still no sign of her after 10 minutes. I call her, but it goes to voice mail.

I ring Sarah on the on call phone. She doesn't answer either.

Another 10 minutes pass.

Constance still doesn't answer.

I ring Sarah and she picks up.

"Hi Sarah, Constance hasn't arrived yet for our double up with Gladys. She's not answering her phone. Do you know where she is?"

"Oh, erm, no I don't, I'll give her a call then call you back, OK? Can you go in and make a start?" Sarah asks.

"I can't get her out of bed myself, so there isn't much I can do to be honest".

"Just go in and make a start, then I'll call you back, OK?" she says sounding pissed off, abruptly hanging up.

I let myself in, plonk my kit down in the kitchen, and go and see Gladys.

"Morning Gladys, how are you?" I ask her, as she rolls over in the bed.

"Morning Rose, you're running late, aren't you?" she says.

"Yes, sorry about that. I'm waiting for Constance, I think she's been held up with another client. I'm not sure how long she will be. Sarah said she'll give me a call back and let me know. She's asked me to come in and make a start", I tell her.

Gladys chuckles, and says, "well, unless you've grown super muscles, there's not much you can do before she gets here! I guess you can put the kettle on and fold some laundry while you wait!"

"OK, see you in a bit", I say, smiling, and head to the kitchen.

I sort and fold the laundry from the dryer and make Gladys a cuppa.

Sarah calls.

"Constance is in another call in Wednesfield at the moment, she's going to be about half an hour. Will you ask Gladys if she wants a bed bath today? Thanks", she says, hanging up before I get a chance to answer.

I take Gladys her cuppa and tell her the news.

"I don't want a bed bath, no. I want to get on the toilet, my pad is soaking!"

I sigh, and say, "I know, I'm sorry about this, Glad!"

"It isn't your fault, Rose. They just don't organise things very well at your place, do they?" she chuckles.

"Doesn't seem like it, does it?" I say.

"Well, I can't stay like this much longer, Rose. If you bring the rotunda over here, and you support my back, I should be able to just manage to get myself up", she says.

"Glad, I don't think its a good idea, I don't want you to hurt yourself!"
"Rose, you know as well as I do that nobody's going to come for a very long time. I can't stay like this!" she says.
I take a moment to think about it.
I shouldn't do this. I should refuse and wait for another carer.
But on the other hand, my client is uncomfortable, and will remain uncomfortable until she's out of bed.
I fetch the rotunda and place it in front of her, place the wheelchair behind it, help her slide her legs round, then support her back as she sits up.
Gladys pulls herself up, me supporting her back, then once she's ready, I turn it till it locks into position with the wheelchair directly behind her, assist her lowering herself into the chair, then wheel her into the bathroom.
Once she's on the toilet safely, I rush round changing the bed sheets, getting fresh clothes out, making tea and cereal, moving the rotunda into the lounge, putting the TV on, putting the washer on, then once she's ready, I assist her with her wash, applying her creams, getting dressed, wheel her into the lounge, get her comfortable in her chair, serve breakfast, open all the curtains, scribble quickly in the care notes, ring out, grab my kit and head off 30 minutes late to my second call.
I text Constance and tell her not to worry about Gladys as I've already completed her call, and that I'll see her at Phil's.

I apologise to my next client for being late. She has already started her wash and tells me not to worry, just to help her finish off.

"You seem stressed out!" she remarks as I pass her a towel.

"I just hate being late, that's all! I think I'll live!" I tell her, all smiles.

"You're in the wrong bloody job then, love! You lot are always late!" she says, laughing.

"I know, terrible, isn't it?"

Once my client is washed, dressed, and sat down eating breakfast, I scribble care notes quickly and leave, hoping to get to Phil as close to on time as possible.

I park up outside, just 15 minutes late.

No sign of Constance.

I give her a call.

"Alright, Rose?" she answers, shouting over the road noise as she's put me on speaker phone whilst she's driving.

"Hiya, I'm at Phil's. Where you at?" I ask her.

"Mate, I don't even know. Somewhere on the A449. I'm following the sat nav, should be there in 10. I'm coming!"

I laugh and say, "alright, see you in a bit!" and hang up.

I go and knock the door.

Debbie answers.

"I knew the good timekeeping wouldn't last!" she says, smiling.

"Morning, Deb! Just me at the moment, Constance is on her way to us now, should be 10 minutes. Thought I'd let you know." I say.

79

"Do you want to come in and wait for her? I know you're not supposed to without the other, but I'm harmless!"
"Thanks Deb, but if its alright with you, I'm gonna have a crafty fag round the corner while I wait for her, because the way this morning's going, I'm not gonna get another chance to have one!"
Debbie laughs and says, "I don't blame you! Get your breaks while you can!"
"OK, see you in a bit!" I say, and dash around the corner to light up my ciggie.

It starts to drizzle rain as I chain smoke two cigarettes and sip my coffee in the cool air.
I pop a mint into my mouth and spray a light mist of perfume onto myself as Constance pulls up next to me.
She jumps out with gloves and aprons, rolls her eyes and says, "Oh my days! This morning is crazy!"
"And it's only just started!" I reply, turning to walk towards the house.
"It's about to get crazier! Someone else has phoned in sick."
"Oh, for fuck's sake!" I mutter under my breath.
"I'll tell you about it after. Just keep smiling, Rose! Keep smiling!" she laughs.

We get Phil sorted in just under 40 minutes, then discuss our new rotas, swap 6 clients, then head off in opposite directions.
It is now 9.45am.
I am determined to finish by 2pm.

I have 4 hours and 15 minutes to get these calls done, and all of them are supposed to be 30 minute calls.
I have to condense 7 hours of work into 4 hours and 15 minutes, so I am going to have to do some serious call cutting.
Constance is in the same boat, along with everybody else.
But never mind.
Sarah is sat in her warm office at her desk with her fan heater and chocolate stash and supply of coffee.
She won't come out to help cover calls. She will just pressure Sue into doing it instead and say that she is 'too busy' even though the ten other staff in the office are more than capable of answering phones, emails,and talking to the care staff and clients.
But anyway...

I rush through the next 7 morning calls, getting 3 clients washed and dressed, making 7 breakfasts, administering 5 sets of medication, applying 4 creams, feeding 4 pets, making 6 cups of tea and 1 coffee, putting 2 loads of washing on, washing up 4 times, filling 1 bird feeder, changing 2 incontinence pads, turning on 5 TV sets, shaving time off of all my calls, and then a quick 5 minute cigarette and coffee break taking me up to 12.16.

I power through the following 7 calls, cutting some to just 11 minutes, making 7 lunches, administering 3 sets of medication, making 5 cups of tea, 1 coffee and 1 hot chocolate,

putting 1 load of laundry in the dryer, changing 3 incontinence pads, washing up 5 times, changing 2 TV channels, in and out, no time for much conversation, and finish at 3.04pm.
If I genuinely had had a doctor's appointment, I wouldn't have made it.
I give Constance a call to see how she's getting on.
"Hi Rose, you alright?" she asks.
"Yeah, I'm good thanks," I say, lighting a cigarette, "how are you getting on?"
"Just two more to go!" she laughs, "man, I'm so hungry right now! I'm microwaving a curry for Mr Johnson, and it smells so good, I want some! But I'll have to wait till I get back, which feels like it's gonna be never!"
"I've done all mine, do you want me to take one of yours?" I ask her.
"Are you sure?" she asks.
"Yeah, who've you got?"
"Mrs James and Mrs Anderson. Who do you want?"
"I'll take Mrs Anderson, I've not had her for a while", I tell her, "it'll be nice to see how she is."
"Alright then, cheers Rose! You're a star!"
"No worries, see you soon!"
"See you!" she says, and hangs up.

I finish my cigarette, then head over to Coven to see Mrs Anderson.
Coven is on the way home for me, and I'm late going home anyway, so why not?

Mrs Anderson lives on a caravan site, and requires assistance onto the commode and a meal making.
We chatter away about her grandchildren, and her daughter's messy divorce whilst I prepare her lunch, scribble in the book, make her a cuppa, and then I head home.

I arrive home at 4.01pm, kiss Pete as I go in, help myself to a large glass of red wine, and go sit outside to drink and smoke a cigarette. My hands shake as I lift up the glass to my lips.
I've been tense all day, rushing around and stressing about traffic, getting soaked in the rain, and I haven't eaten anything all day.
Pete comes out and asks me what I'd like for dinner.
"Can we have fish and chips, please, with baked beans or peas?" I ask him as he bends down to kiss me.
"Yes. Are you making it?" He asks.
"I can if you don't want to", I reply, hoping I don't have to get up.
"I'm just really tired honey, I didn't sleep well, can you do it, please?" he says.
I sigh, then nod and get up.
It isn't hard to bang the food into the oven, I just really can't be bothered after my shift.
I sit down with Pete and my wine outside in the cold air, not feeling like I'm really there, chatting about bikes that he's been looking at on the internet and me briefly telling him about my day.
I feel like I live at work, and that I am only visiting when I am at home.

All I think about is work.
All I do is work.
I prioritise my client calls over my social plans.
I work over my shift to help out my fellow care workers instead of rushing home to enjoy my free time.
Free time?
I did just say free time, didn't I?
Well, these days my free time is either spent asleep, or showering, or eating, or doing laundry, falling asleep in front of the TV, or arguing with Pete and my friends because I am always at work and am neglecting my relationships and myself and never want to do anything or go anywhere or have a life and I'm so tired that I don't even notice that I don't have a life anymore, etc.
But it will be Friday soon enough, and I will have my job interview, and I will kick ass in it, and if the company seems better than the one I currently work with, I'll take the job and leave after Christmas.
Oh, how I want to leave this horrible, heartless company!

Once the food is ready, I serve up, scoff it quickly, wash it down with more wine and head straight to bed.
I've barely spoken to Pete, and I know he's annoyed with me. He wanted me to go with him to visit his friends next week but I'd already agreed to work an extra shift and now he will be going alone.
I feel bad that we never spend time together anymore, but what am I to do? I'm the only one working at the moment, and the bills are

mounting up, I'm living in my overdraft, and it seems that the more I work, the less money I have. It all goes straight back out onto petrol and the additional vehicle maintenance due to covering so many miles for work purposes that the servicing intervals seem to come up every couple months.
I'll be out the house for 18 hours a day, and be paid for maybe 12.
We end up earning below the minimum wage because they get away with not paying us for the time spent traveling between clients, even though it is for work purposes.
No wonder there's a shortage of care workers. Who wants to work this hard for free?
I'm beginning to understand why many healthcare staff date or are married to other healthcare staff. Nobody else could understand the demands of this kind of work without doing it themselves.
I just hope that Pete doesn't go anywhere.

I wake up on Friday morning, shower, blow dry my hair, put on subtle makeup, a nice jumper dress and leggings, knee high boots, and look in the mirror.
Damn, I look good today.
I'm gonna kick ass at this interview!
Pete kisses me and tells me I look great, and gives me a pep talk over coffee whilst I chain smoke and he warms up his bike.
He's going to drop me off and wait in the cafe round the back.
I'm not even slightly nervous.
I know I'll get this job. I'm a very employable person.

I'm only doubting whether I want it or not.
They pay more per hour, but what if this company is as much of a shambles as the one I'm currently at?
Well, they are based closer to my house and pay more, so it will be a stepping stone I guess.

I arrive 20 minutes early, and have a cigarette in the parking lot.
Pete gives me another pep talk whilst I put my fag out, spray perfume and pop a mint into my mouth.
He gives me a kiss and I head to reception.

The receptionist calls someone to collect me.
I'm assuming it will be Marie, who I have arranged the interview with.
It is not Marie who collects me.
It is a Man called Ben.
I follow him into the office where he asks me to take a seat.
I sit for a while, looking at the Christmas decorations that have been put up.
It seems much more relaxed in this office than my current company's office, for example, the phones haven't rang in the last 5 minutes I've been here, and nobody is on the phone begging staff to cover shifts and client calls.
That's a good sign.
Ben asks me if I am here for the Care Worker role or Care Coordinator role.
Fucking De Ja Vu.
This is exactly what happened at my company.
Went to the interview, nobody was expecting me, nobody knew what I was there for.

Ha.
I tell him the Care Worker vacancy.
He asks me my name again, has a whisper with a colleague, makes another phone call, then offers me a coffee and apologises that the person supposed to be interviewing me is currently off sick, but somebody will be with me in about 15 minutes.
Ha.
This is perhaps *not* a good sign.
I sip Ben's shit coffee and wait.

15 minutes later, a lady bursts into the office, dumps her bag on a desk, downs a cup of coffee, throws the Costa cup in the bin, rips off her scarf and throws it on a chair, then rushes over to me to shake my hand.
"Hi Rose, I'm Claudia. Sorry about your wait. Would you like to come through?" She asks, opening a door into an office.
The interview goes very well. I have Claudia in hysterics for most of it, when she asks me for an example of an occasion where I've worked under pressure and how I dealt with it.
I laugh and tell her, "every day!" and go on to tell her in a lighthearted manner about the situations I've found myself in, the unrealistic workloads, and throwing back questions to her about this company.
I ask about their rotas, their staff retention, and she reassures me that they are set out very well, with 5 minutes travel time in between calls, and says that staff don't leave this branch, that they are happy and all work together well on regular runs.

She reassures me that I won't be expected to travel more than 1.5 miles between calls, that if I was on the Pendeford run, for example, that I would remain in Pendeford for my entire shift.
This is music to my ears!
The training is paid, the 2 weeks of shadow shifts are also paid.
At my current company, it was not paid.
Again, music to my ears!
She says that the next training is next week.
Then offers me the job.
I tell her that I need to give one month's notice to my current employer, and ask when the next training is so that I'll be able to give the correct notice period.
She says she will find out for me and email me later today when she finds out.
Wicked.

I leave the office full of smiles, feeling positive that I'll be able to escape soon.
I go round the back to the parking lot, light a ciggie and call Pete.
He comes out to me with a takeout coffee for me.
"How did it go?" He asks me.
"Well, I got the job, obviously," I say.
"Well? Do they seem any good?"
I tell him all about the interview, and everything that was said, that it sounds better and have been assured that they are much more efficient than my company.
He hugs me and kisses me.
"Well done, honey, I'm proud of you!" he says.

We go home, make love, and watch a film together. I'm on a late shift tomorrow so I can stay up and enjoy some quality time with my man for a change.
We drink wine and cuddle on the sofa until I fall asleep.

Five

Absolute, utter bullshit!
Aargh!
I went to have a meeting with Sarah, and I told her how exhausted I am, and how I'm not getting enough rest between shifts.
I told her that the stress is really getting to me, and how I simply cannot cope with such a massive, unreasonable workload of covering 4 areas in 1 shift - areas which are between 5 and 15 miles away from each other - with NO time to travel between them, No time for breaks, and constantly running well over an hour late to ALL of my client calls.
I told Sarah that it is NOT SAFE for me as a Care Worker, or for my clients, who need to have their medications and meals ON TIME, and reminded her that having care staff running around on empty like we all are, so tired and worn down, is making staff MISS THINGS, like when one of our clients wasn't given the correct medication last week because a new member of staff was so worn out and rushed that she FORGOT to hand over the client's tablets that she'd just laid out in the kitchen ready, and how another member of staff CRASHED HER CAR three days ago

because she was so run down that she fell asleep at the wheel.

I told Sarah that ALL OF US need things to change before something worse happens, like one of the clients ending up dead.

And do you know what she said?

Nothing.

Sweet, fuck all.

She just... Blinked at me.

Blank expression.

What the fuck is that?

And *then* she had the cheek to ask me if I'd work tonight.

How I didn't swing for her, I'll never know!

So yeah, the meeting went well.

Bunch of bastards, the lot of them.

I don't even recognise Sue anymore.

Sue used to stick up for us, help out when she could, but now?

Now she's been worn down so much by Sarah and the pressures and stresses, that she's even beginning to sound like her.

You know, it is winter, and the roads are icy. Last week, I went to turn a corner on my motorcycle, and the back wheel skidded on the ice, and I came off.

I wasn't too hurt, but the impact bent my handlebars making it unrideable and I smashed an indicator.

I'd hit my head, but my crash helmet took the blow. I felt stiff and my knee was hurt where the bike landed on it.

A man in the car behind me helped me to pick up my bike and park on the road side.

I called Sue and told her what had happened, that I had to call the breakdown services to

collect my bike and said I needed to get medical attention as my neck felt stiff and I was limping as I'd injured my knee.
Do you know what she did?
She sent another Care Worker to come and pick me up. Not to see if I was OK, but to take me to my next double up call at Phil and Debbie's.
The Care Worker, Julie, told me that Sue had said I'd broken down.
Julie was absolutely disgusted when she saw I was injured and found out that I'd had an accident but was still expected to work.
She called Sue at the client's house.
Debbie made me a coffee, bless her, and told me not to worry, that she'd help Julie with Phil, and called an ambulance for me.
Julie was fuming when she got off the phone to Sue.
"She doesn't even give a shit!", Julie had said, "she doesn't care, she only cares about getting the calls covered!"
I just sat and cried.
After Julie had gone on to her next call, and Debbie had looked after me, and the ambulance crew had been and gone, advising only that my blood pressure seemed high (which I'd laughed at - I said it was the stress of this job), Pete came to pick me up.
My bike went into the workshop for a couple days.
Sue and Sarah put me on double up shifts for a couple days so I didn't have to drive, and both asked me how my bike was.
How is the bike?
Not, how is Rose?

Yep. That pretty much sums it all up.
Well, I've got another job to go to. My training starts in mid January, so I'll be handing in my resignation today.
I am SO done with this bullshit company!

It has been a week since I handed in my letter of resignation, and Sarah hasn't even said anything at all to me about it, but I know she's received it, as within an hour of dropping it in, I received a text message from Sue asking if I was leaving.
Yes, I am leaving, and I can't bloody wait!
It will be Christmas next week, and I am working over the entire period with a promise of double pay, then I will work over New Year, then just 2 weeks of January before I walk straight into training with me new company with better pay, and hopefully better working conditions.
I just want to get this last stretch over and done with, to be honest.
So many of my colleagues have asked me when I'm leaving, all saying that they are leaving too, or that they want to.
The thing is, I haven't actually told anyone other than Sarah that I'm leaving.
I feel quite amused at how quickly the gossip has spread.
You see, us Care Workers don't tend to have much of a social life due to the busy and demanding nature of our work, so all we really have to talk about is each other.
I mean, hardly any of us have the time or energy to even watch television, so we only

really get to watch it when our clients have it on in the background, watching soap operas and the news.

That is the only way I can keep up with current affairs.

Some of my clients watch quiz shows, and when I'm scribbling in the care notes, I sometimes try and answer the questions, making my clients laugh because I often get them wrong.

One of my favourite clients, Jean, likes to watch the rally car racing. She loves it. Quite often, when I go round to her, she'll have it on, or be listening to classic rock on the radio.

Jean is awesome. She never asks for anything, and so I always go the extra mile for her, doing her ironing, going to the shop for her, picking up her favourite mocha drinks from the cheap shops by me when I go to get my own shopping, watering her plants, little things which aren't on the Care Plan, but that I like to do.

Because she never asks for anything, other staff tend to be in and out in 5 minutes, not even stopping for a chat.

Now, Jean doesn't like making a fuss. She doesn't want to be a burden to anyone, so she doesn't really like to ask for things. But because I stay and chat with her, watching the rally car racing, she has opened up a little and tells me her worries about her brother, and how her hair has been falling out, how she's too afraid to go outside to peg the washing out in case she has another fall, how she wants us to help her to have a shave every now and then, because her chin is starting to get hairy and she felt too embarrassed to ask.

Part of this job is supposed to be to befriend our clients, building positive, healthy working relationships.

You wouldn't think that reading some of the care notes in the client folders, and I'm not referring to just Jean's now, but I'll write Jean as the client's name.

This is a pretty standard extract from a rushed, overworked Care Assistant in a client folder:

'Jean fine on arrival. Made cup of tea and 2x toast. Washed, dressed, creamed feet, gave meds, had a chat, all fine on leave'.

Was 'Jean' fine on arrival? Was the client asked if they were fine? Did the client actually state that they were fine, or did the member of staff just assume they were fine because they were awake and breathing with the telly on?

Did 'Jean' make the cup of tea and toast, or did the member of staff?

Did the client get themselves washed and dressed, or did the worker assist? Or was the worker stating that the client was already washed and dressed when they got there?

What cream went on the client's feet?

What medication was given?

What did they chat about? Was it an actual chat, or was it a standard 'you alright, Jean? Yeah? Good' two or three sentence exchange?

Was everything fine on leave? Did the client have access to a drink or snack?

Had the client eaten the toast and drank the tea? Or was it left on the table for them?

This is an example of what the care notes *should have* read:

'I let myself in with the key from the key safe. Jean was sat in her armchair in the lounge watching TV on arrival. She said she was fine. I assisted her in the shower. Jean washed her face, arms and torso. I assisted washing her back, legs, feet and bottom.
I assisted her drying and dressing. Jean chose a pink blouse and cream trousers to wear, and brushed her teeth. I assisted styling her hair, and applied E45 cream to her feet.
Jean said that she would like a cup of tea and 2x toast with butter for her breakfast, so I made these for her, and administered her medication (3x tablets from blister pack) which she took with a glass of water.
She was eating her breakfast back in her armchair in the lounge whilst watching TV. We had a chat. Jean said that she was feeling a little under the weather with a headache, but was looking forward to her brother visiting her later on today.
I left a glass of water on the table for her for later.
Jean was still eating breakfast in the lounge upon leave.'

These care notes go to social services and help them to review client care packages. If, for example, 'Jean' had been requiring more assistance than usual over a period of 12 weeks, they would be able to see this in the care notes and possibly extend the amount of care the client receives.

If 'Jean' was becoming more independent, then perhaps she would require less care services.

If care staff are writing vague notes, it is hard to tell whether the client is getting all of their needs met or not.

However, I get why staff are writing less and less. When you have to be in and out, are running extremely late, and have another 14 clients to attend to within the next 6 hours, every minute counts. Writing notes tends to take between 2-8 minutes, depending on whether a client is having their bowel movements and urine output charted, whether you have to sign off all the medication, whether their fluid and food intake is being monitored, whether skin integrity (pressure sores, cuts, bruising etc) is being monitored, and if you only have 30 minutes to wash, dress, cream, feed and water a client, you don't have 8 minutes to spend on notes and charting.

This is an ongoing issue with Social Services, who still expect a care worker to be able to assist with continence care, *and* prepare a meal, *and* give medication within as little as 15 minutes.

How can anyone provide an effective service in so little time?

I start my shift in Bishop's Wood at 6.30am. It is foggy, dark, and very icy.

The pavements glitter as I walk up my client's driveway, fighting with a key safe with numb hands and gripping my torch between my teeth so that I can actually bloody see what I'm doing.

I eventually gain access and have to gently wake my client, Sabrina.

"Morning Sabrina, it's Rose," I gently whisper, and switch on the lamp next to the bed.

"Rose, what time is it?" she grumbles.

"It's half six", I tell her.

"Oh man, why is it so early!" she complains, rubbing her eyes and looking at me from her bed, "they don't normally come till seven!"

"I'm sorry, they've put you as my first call today," I tell her.

"OK, let's get it over with!" she says, using her bed remote to make her back sit up. She has a drink of water from her glass on the table and swallows her tablets, and says, "Get me my chair and my towel."

I help Sabrina out of her nightie, position her wheelchair next to the bed so that she can slide herself across, wrap her towel around her, then switch the shower on so that it will warm up whilst she takes herself to the toilet. I give her some privacy and prep the kitchen to make breakfast, then start scribbling in the care notes.

Sabrina calls me back in, and I assist her onto the shower chair, where she washes herself and we have a laugh discussing her brother's hot friend that she's trying to seduce.

Once she's finished, I help her dry her back and bottom, and into her clothes.

She always wears stunning clothes, a mix of traditional Indian and Western styles, and does her makeup everyday.

She has cereal for breakfast, and puts the news on the TV in the sitting room while I finish scribbling my notes.

"Where are you working today then, Rose?" she asks.

"I've got two more up here, then I'm in Coven, then back up here for one call, then a few in Penkridge."

"Why do they make you all go back and forth for? It's stupid!" she says, taking another mouthful.

"They like to keep us on our toes!" I say.

She laughs, and says, "either that, or they're just thick, right?"

I laugh too.

"Oh, Rose, have you got Ali on your rota today? You know, the one with the fit son?" she asks.

"Sabrina, you know I can't talk about other clients!"

"You're not, though! It's a client's fit son! He's called Sukdeep or something, and he's only up the A5 a bit from here. He's not married! I asked Ali when I saw him at play group!" she says.

I burst out laughing and say, "Play group? What's that?"

"The spinal injuries group we go to," she giggles, "that's what I've nicknamed it!"

"Bloody hell!" I say, coughing from laughing so hard.

"You know me, little miss inappropriate! That's why I haven't found a husband yet, isn't it?

It's not the wheelchair that puts them off, it's my mouth!"

I manage to stop laughing and close the care folder.

"I've gotta go. I've not got him today, anyway", I tell her, and stand up.

"When you do see him, tell him to tell that hunk of a son that I said hello!" she says, still giggling.

"Yeah, OK, I'm gonna leave now! Tell him yourself when you see him at Play Group!" I say, and burst into laughter again.

I sign out on my phone app, and check my personal phone.

6 missed calls and 2 text messages.

I call Sandra, the other care worker I'm on with today.

She answers sounding very pissed off.

"Rose, thank God! Where are you?" she says.

"I'm in Bishop's Wood. What's up?"

"Me and you have to cover Doreen's shift between us, on top of our other calls!" she shouts.

"OK, calm down. What areas are they?" I ask.

"They're in Codsall, Brewood, Coven, and Perton. How the fuck are we meant to do it? We've got double up calls in between, and no travel time as it is!"

"Shit, OK, hang on," I say, and pause to think before answering, "we've got a double up in Bishop's Wood next. Text me the client list, come up here, we'll get the double up done, if you take the Coven calls, I'll do Codsall, we can meet back here for the double up, I'll do Brewood, then I'm in Penkridge. When you get here we'll look at our rotas and see what we can do and maybe swap some stuff around. Is anyone else helping?"

"No, they're all off sick. Sarah's not answering, and Sue's in Wombourne so she can't help. This is gonna be a shit shift!" Sandra says, sounding teary.

"We can only do what we can do!" I tell her calmly, "Get up here and we'll sort it out. Where are you now?"

"I'm 20 minutes away", she says.

"OK, I'll go do my single call, and I'll see you in a bit" I say and hang up.

I read my texts and see that Gina has sent an angry message that she's also covering extra calls, going between Wolverhampton and Penkridge. I reply to her and tell her we can't help as we're doing Doreen's shift as well as our own.

Today is going to be really, really shit.

Oh well.

Sandra meets me at the double up. We get the client sorted out, then discuss rotas in the country lane round the corner from the farmhouse, both of us desperately puffing away on our cigarettes.

We swap calls around, hoping that for the three double ups we have, that we will be able to meet at roughly the same time at the same place.

Sandra heads to Coven and I head to Codsall. I fly through 5 client visits, shaving time off where I can, getting 3 washed and dressed, giving 4 sets of medication, changing 2 incontinence pads, making 5 breakfasts, 4 cups of tea and 1 coffee, feeding 1 pet, emptying 2 commodes, and speeding down the country lanes back up to Bishop's Wood for our double up.

We change the client's pad, and apply barrier cream to her bottom, then reposition her onto her other side.

The client's family take care of the rest. Sandra and I again swap client calls whilst puffing away down the lane. She has more calls in Coven and agrees to do the calls in Perton, whilst I cover Brewood and Penkridge. We are both tired and stressed, and she says that she wants to leave.

"You know, I started a week before you," she tells me, "and I thought that this would be a nice job, helping people in the community, and all that. This is not a nice job, though, is it?"

"I think that it could be a nice job, if it was run better," I reply, "I mean, if we actually had enough time to do the work, and had support from management, and enough sleep between shifts, then we wouldn't all be off sick all the while, or stressed out, and we'd all be happy and do our jobs better!"

We both laugh.

"Aint gonna happen any time soon though, is it?" she says.

"Doesn't look like it," I say, and sigh.

"You're leaving. Everyone's leaving." she says.

"Yep. I'm hoping that there are better companies out there."

"Anything's better that this!" she says.

We part ways and crack on with our mental day.

I cover 4 calls in Brewood, still making breakfasts at 12.45 in the afternoon, then head to Penkridge for 6 lunch calls, finishing at 3.20pm.

I call Sandra to see how she's doing. She's just finishing up at the last call in Perton.

"I've gotta pay out another £40 to my babysitter now, because I'm supposed to be home already! So most of today's wages have been for nothing!" she says angrily.

"Oh fucking hell! That really sucks, San!" I say, feeling bad for her.

"It happens all the time though, Rose! I can't remember the last time I got home on time! They don't care in the office, that I've got 3 kids to feed, and that being forced to work over my shift puts me in a position where I have childcare issues and end up paying out most of my wages on extra childcare. It's shit!"

"It is shit, you're right. Try and get out, if you can!" I say to her.

"I'm gonna, trust me! I'm done with this bullshit!" she says.

We say goodbye and I head home to my frustrated partner, who was expecting me back 3 hours ago and had made me lunch, which was now cold and soggy in the microwave.

Pete and I have a brief argument about communication and how I should always let him know if I'm going to be late back no matter how rushed I am, as it only takes a minute to send a fucking text message, and I

need to start doing it as he worries that I'm dead in a ditch down a country lane and so on, and I just nod and head straight to the fridge to get my wine.
Bad girlfriend, Rose!
This is what I do, now.
I go home, drink wine to try and relax, neglect my partner because I'm too tired to interact with him, and sleep.
If it was the other way around with Pete and I swapping roles, I'd be seriously considering whether or not I was wasting my time with this relationship.
I don't want him to leave me, but right now I have no fight left in me to try and encourage him to stay, should he decide enough's enough.
I just plod on and hope that once the next few weeks are over, that I'll have time and energy to make it all up to him.
If only I had the energy to communicate this with him!
But I don't, and so I just drink my wine, eat my soggy lunch, cry, and fall asleep.

Six

It is Christmas Eve, and my rota looks promising of an easy, straightforward shift.
This can't be right, can it?
Saying that, quite a few clients are with family members over the festive period and have canceled their calls, so for once, the pressure is off.
Great stuff.

Today I am covering Coven and Codsall, then 3 calls in Penkridge.
11 easy calls, where I am actually familiar with *all* of my clients, so it should be a nice run.
I knock off the first three calls all in the same building in 47 minutes, then head to the lady 5 streets away and get her ready for the day in 26 minutes.
I'm running early.
Great! Time for a quick ciggie and some coffee!
Off to Codsall, where my 4 clients are easy peasy to get ready, and I even have time to have a coffee with my one client, and a good giggle about how we hate Christmas and say we'll both be wearing our 'Bah, Humbug' hats tomorrow.
My 3 lunch calls in Penkridge are also easy, and so once my last lady is sat down eating her microwave meal, I head home not just on time, but actually, early!
Pete is shocked to see me get home so soon. He pours me a glass of wine, and we make chicken fajitas together for our lunch, and enjoy a nice cuddle in bed with a DVD on.
Later on, we make love, twice!
I also apologise to him for being so horrible lately.
I fall asleep in his arms.

Christmas day.
My rota says that I will be in Penkridge all shift.
The entire shift, in the same town.
Even gaps in the rota!
Great stuff!

Pete isn't particularly happy that I'm working today, as he wanted us to spend the day together, and for it to be special.
I told him we'd have all evening together, but he still isn't happy, as I have an early start tomorrow with a full 16 hour shift.
But still, it's double time!
Think of the money, Rose!
My shift flows smoothly, and I even get to drink *all* of my coffee in my flask, *and* eat my cereal bars, before the end of my shift.
The little village centre is completely dead, just the odd car passing through.
I finish at 12pm as the last call is canceled, and I arrive home at 12.30, with plenty time for Pete and I to open our gifts, share some wine, watch a DVD and make sweet, sweet love.
We even manage to have a shower together.
Lovely.

Boxing day.
I'm warming up my bike and hear the clunky clunk noise of my rota updating.
I knew it wouldn't last.
Today I am now covering Featherstone, Penkridge, Coven, Bishop's Wood, Brewood, Willenhall and Wednesfield.
Fucking wonderful.
22 client calls, back to back, some a 40 minute drive away from each other.
No breaks for me today, then!
Right, let's get it over with.

I have 1 call in Featherstone, a quick in and out, make a cup of tea and toast, then a 35 minute drive to Penkridge, but having no travel time, I arrive 35 minutes late to my first call, Gladys, which is a double up with Sue, but Sue has already done pretty much everything, so I help her finish up, and run 25 minutes late to my next client.

The call lasts a full 30 minutes with my client who has dementia. She had forgotten why I was helping her to undress and had a bit of a panic, but I managed to calm her down.

I am 30 minutes late to client 4. I manage to shave 10 minutes off the call, and run 23 minutes late to client 5.

Client 5 is Betty, who is refusing to eat her breakfast or take her medication, and she is very agitated. Thankfully, Betty's Dementia Nurse, Claire, arrives and helps me to calm her and she takes her medication in the end.

I run 40 minutes late to client 6 due to traffic. I apologise profusely, but my client says that he's so used to it now, anything under an hour late is early in his eyes.

I run 50 minutes late to client 7. She has wet the bed as she has been unable to get herself up and onto the commode. She is not happy at all, and says that she's sick of our excuses. She says that for over a month we have all been letting her down, and how she feels that she has no dignity now, as she can't hold her bladder for long, and if we were on time, she wouldn't be wetting herself on a daily basis and having to suffer the humiliation that she feels.

I apologise more, but she just shrugs and tells me that none of us really care.

"Why do you bother apologising?" she says, "you're not sorry, you don't care, you're still getting paid at the end of the day!"

"I am sorry, and I do care. I'm sorry that you've had to put up with appalling service over the last few weeks. In your care folder, there is a complaints form that you can fill in, or you can call the office should you wish to complain, because you shouldn't be waiting this long every day. It isn't good enough." I tell her calmly, whilst helping her to get dressed.

She doesn't say much after that, but seems to calm down a bit now that she knows she's been heard.

I run 55 minutes late to client 8, and manage to shave 13 minutes off the call.

I'm 45 minutes late to client 9, who says he isn't bothered, he just wants his marmalade on toast and a nice cup of tea.

I shave 10 minutes off of his call and arrive 39 minutes late to client 10.

Client 10 is a double up call, but Sue, my second carer, has not arrived yet.

"Where are you?" I ask her when she answers.

"I'm in fucking Willenhall. Go do your next single call and I'll meet you back there after, OK?" she says.

"Alright. In a bit" I hang up.

I'm 45 minutes late to client 11, but she tells me that she is just happy that someone has turned up. I help her on and off the toilet, and make her some lunch.

Back to Client 10, Sue pulls up as I take my helmet off, and we shave 10 minutes off the call.

I am 1 hour 10 minutes late to client 12, another client who bites my head off as he is also sick of our excuses for running late.
"Everyone's always off sick! There's always traffic! There's always a poorly client! Get some more bloody staff, then!" he shouts.
"I am sorry for being so late, but I'm here now and I would like to do my job. What would you like for your lunch?" I calmly ask.
I manage to fly through his call in 15 minutes, have a quick ciggie and drink some coffee, and get to client 13 bang on time.
I was supposed to have 1 hour 30 minutes break between shifts. That has not been possible, but at least I am on time now.
This shift consists of all double up calls, and I'm on with Gina, so I leave my bike on the road and jump in the car with her for the rest of the shift.
"So you'm leaving, then?" she asks me as she drives to our next call.
"Yeah, just two more weeks to go!" I say, smiling.
"I'm going, too. They just promoted me to Team Leader, yeah? But for the sake of an extra twenty pence an hour, I have to organise fifteen carers, and if they can't do a shift, I have to do the shift. I also get a a bonus monthly is none of my team is off sick, but out of 15 carers, there's always at least 2 off in any month, so its just them in the office trying to get all the calls covered and get Team Leaders to hassle all the staff to work extra instead of them having to do it. It's a load of bollocks!" she says.
"Sounds like it!" I agree.

"Yeah, cos I'm going to the NHS, and they're paying two pound an hour more than we're on now, and that's to be at the level we're at now. Promoted, and you get more. Plus, I wanna get into nursing, so it will be better for me to have hospital experience, and they actually train you. The training here is a load of bollocks!" she says.

"Yeah, I remember the training! But anyway, Gina, good for you! I'm really pleased for you!" I tell her.

"Thanks, I just can't wait to get out of here! Three weeks for me!"

Gina and I have a good laugh with all our clients, making jokes and being cheery, and after a tough start to the day, I go home feeling better.

The next week flies by, and I do five 16-hour shifts, two 8-hour shifts, have a day off where I spend 14 hours of it asleep, and then go back to work.

This is to be my last week now, and I head up to Bishop's Wood to start my shift with Sabrina.

We chat whilst she showers and I sort her clothes out.

"So, is this your last week, then?" she asks.

"Yes, it is", I say.

"Rose, you're supposed to at least *pretend* to be sad that you're leaving me!" she says with a smile.

"I could pretend, but it's not all about you, you know!" I joke, and she throws a flannel at me.

"You're a cheeky cow, you know!" she giggles, "I bet you can't wait really!"

"Counting the days, innit!", I say, passing her the flannel.

Once she's seated and eating breakfast, I scribble out my notes.

"You know, Rose, if it was me, I'd write in every client's folder, 'Fuck You Sarah' in big capital letters!" Sabrina laughs.

I chuckle, "no, because when Social Services read it, I'll never be able to work in care again!"

"You should just do it anyway, as like, a leaving present to me!" she says.

"I'm the one leaving, why are you getting a leaving gift? Where's mine?" I laugh.

"You get paid to be in my lovely company, that is your gift, isn't it?!" she says, smiling.

"Well, you are special!" I say, trying to hold a serious expression.

"Rose, what d'you mean by that? I'm special? You mean like, special needs? You cheeky bitch!" she giggles.

"Take it whatever way you want!" I laugh.

"It's only you who gets away with playing me up, you know! You always give as good as you get, and I like that. I respect you for it, isn't it? I might miss you, if I get stuck with the miserable carers, you know?" she says.

"Thanks, Sabrina. Nicest thing anyone's ever said to me. You *might* miss me!" I laugh.

"Yeah, I might. Keep up that attitude, missy, and I might not!" she says, smiling.

"Right, I'm gonna bugger off!", I tell her, standing up, "I might see you again before I go. If not, enjoy your miserable carers who will never be as awesome as me!"

"See you, Rose!" she calls as I wave and lock the door behind me.

Clients like Sabrina make my day so much better. I will miss the banter.

I sign off on the app, then look at my updated rota.

For fuck's sake.

I see that I'm supposed to be in Coven right now, even though it is a 20 minute drive away, and then I'm supposed to be in Willenhall, a 40 minute drive away...

I check out my rota for the rest of the week. Tomorrow they want me to go to Wombourne, where I'd actually start in Bridgnorth, then have no travel time to get to Wombourne, to run at least an hour late all day...

Next day, the same. No travel time despite calls being 15 miles away from each other.

I close my eyes and take a deep breath.

I cannot put up with any more of this bullshit rota crap, and for the sake of my own sanity, and respect for myself, I am not doing it.

I refuse.

No more.

I call Sarah, but get Sue instead. I tell her that I am unable to complete the rest of my shift, that cover will need to be arranged, and to not expect me in for the rest of the week.

I then go to my doctor's surgery, see my GP and explain my situation, how stressed out I am, that I cannot face going back to work my last week, and they give me a sick note for my employer.

I then go home, and climb into bed with Pete.

"You're early", he says, half asleep.
"I can't do anymore. I've got a sick note from my GP. I can relax now before I start training for my new job," I tell him, snuggling up to him.
"I think that's very wise," he says, "you can start anew, feeling refreshed."
"Yep, that's the plan!", I agree, and close my eyes.

<u>Seven</u>

I spend my week off catching up with laundry, housework, and going out to places with Pete. He takes me to Bridgnorth for the day, where we go to cafes and a pub by the river, we go shopping in town, and we watch countless films together.
I catch up with a couple friends, enjoy having lie ins, and just relaxing.
I feel free and chilled out for the first time in months.

My week of training with my new company flies by swiftly. Each day, with how in depth the training is on each subject, I realise just how shoddy my last company was. Even having experience in care, along with other members of the group, we all find that we are learning new things.

At the end of the week, I speak to Marie in the office and ask her when I will be starting my shadow shifts.

"Hi Rose, you won't be able to start until we get your reference back from your last company. I have put the request in, and I've spoken to staff in their office who have said they'll get it sorted, so we're just waiting on them."

"OK, no worries," I say, then ask, "I've heard some of the other care staff leaving the branch that they've been refusing to give anyone a reference. Can I give you another employer? Or a character reference?"

"No, because it's your only care related reference, and with it being so recent, we need that one, I'm afraid. Maybe if you speak to your old manager, they'll be able to chase it up for you?" she says.

"I'll call and find out", I say, smiling.

I leave, smoking a cigarette as I walk to my bike in the car park, feeling really pissed off. I've had a great week off, and a great week of training, and now I have to wait for those bastards in the office at my old job who are stopping me from starting my new job and moving forward.

I'd been warned by Gina that they were doing this, to try and force staff to come back to them.

Well, they can fuck off!

I head home and have a bitch to Pete about it all, and he comforts me, orders takeout, and gives me wine.

I'm stressing that I'll have no work for a while, so I jump on the laptop and apply for 23 care vacancies across the West Midlands.
I need to do something!

I spend the weekend applying for countless jobs, mainly bank staff vacancies, seeing as I may be starting my new job at any time.
As it turns out, a lot of care companies advertise bank staff positions, but only actually have full time positions available and don't do bank staff.
9 of the 13 companies I called, inquiring about their bank staff vacancies, told me that.
What the fuck!
Why advertise it, then?
Whatever.
Move on, Rose!

Monday morning, I've had an email from a care home in Birmingham, asking me to call to arrange an interview.
I'm surprised that they want to interview me, as the advert I applied to stated that they wanted at least 1 year of care experience, and qualified to level 3 in health and social.
I have 5 months experience of care, and am at level 2.
Perhaps they are scraping the barrel.
Either way, I need a job.
I call and arrange an interview for Thursday.
I also arrange an appointment at the Job Centre for Friday, as I have no idea when I will actually be starting work, and I will run out of money within a month.

It is Thursday, and Pete is going to take me to my interview.
I put on a black suit that I know I look really hot in, do subtle makeup, and we head off.
Traffic is horrendous, and then Pete's bike starts spluttering as he had forgotten to fill up.
We just make it to a petrol station, and I call ahead to let them know that I will be running 15 minutes late.
I start to stress a little, but we make it with me only being 10 minutes late.
The interview goes really well.
I have the two managers in hysterics for most of it, being serious when I need to, but generally being my cheery, fun self.
They end up offering me the job, promising that they'll put me through a level 3 Health and Social Care course, plenty of training, 2 weeks paid shadow working, plenty of opportunity for advancement as they are expanding the company and opening a new home, and it all sounds like a good thing.
They just need a DBS check, which could take a few weeks to come through.
I tell them that I'm on the DBS update system, so I can give them the certificate number, and they can just view it online and save themselves fifty quid, but they tell me that they have to do a new one with each employee.
Okey doke.

I leave, feeling great, and head down the road to the pub where Pete is waiting for me.
He buys me a rum and coke, and I tell him all about it.

He's really pleased for me.
I don't know how I feel. I'm pleased I have got 2 jobs, but neither of them I can start yet!
I still have to go to the job centre tomorrow and sort all of that out.
In the mean time, I can afford to pay my rent next month, but nothing else.
I need to be starting work ASAP!
I can't tell you how frustrated I feel, knowing that I could already be working, but my last company not sending my reference - the one thing holding me back - is completely out of my control.
I hate that I can't do anything about it.
I've left several messages with the office, and have been promised that it will get done, but then... Nothing!
Aargh!
Bunch of lying arseholes.
WANKERS!
AARGH!

I sort out my appointment with the Job Centre, who tell me that I won't receive anything for 6 weeks, but am assured by my advisor that it will be backdated.
But I will only receive £574 per month.
This doesn't even cover both my rent and council tax, let alone bills, groceries, petrol etc.
In the mean time, I have fuck all to spend, no groceries in the flat, and no money to pay my bills due in 2 weeks.
In fact, I'm currently in minus figures at the bank, living in my overdraft.

If I am able to start work before the 6 weeks are up, I won't have enough cash to put petrol in my vehicle to even get to work.
This is going to be fun.
Bollocks.

This last month has been absolutely awful.
Pete and I have been arguing pretty much non stop, as he has had to step in to use all of his money to buy all of our groceries, and I've had to borrow some from him, which I can't really afford to pay back, but there you go.
He has been so kind and generous, and I have been... argumentative, resentful, embarrassed that I've had to accept his help when I have *never* had to rely on anybody else, and have *always* been *completely* self-sufficient.
My bad mood isn't anything to do with him, it's just me and all of my crap in my head.
I never ask for help, or admit when I actually need help, so for me to have to actually go to somebody else for help and support, has really been tough for me, and I have taken out my frustrations on him a little bit.
OK, well, a lot.
I have apologised, but I think I hurt him when I tried to explain to him that I find it hard to accept help.
I think that he felt that it was me not placing trust in him.
I don't know.
Maybe.
Who knows.
Pete knows, but Rose doesn't know.
Whatever.

Let's move on.

So yeah, I've been out of work for 6 weeks in total, and I'm behind on ALL of my bills, including rent.

I now have no deposit as my landlord has used that for rent payment.

I am -£650 in one bank account, and -£120 in the other.

I owe the electric company £340 from over the winter period where they got my meter readings the wrong way round and decided to land me with that nice bill once they had put them right.

I owe Pete £100 for groceries and petrol.

My last company STILL have not sent over a fucking reference for me.

But hey, good news, I've started my new job in the care home!

Aaand I hate it already.

Not the job, just the other staff.

Well, some of them.

Basically, I started three days ago, and I'm on shadow shifts with the other carers for two weeks.

I'm supposed to be being shown who is who, what to do and when, the residents' routines, where everything is kept, what is expected of me, etc.

All I am getting is, 'Oh, you've got experience in care? Great! You'll be fine!'.

When asking where things are kept, I get, 'Oh, don't worry, you'll pick it up!' instead of a fucking answer.

When I ask about their systems in the medication room for residents' medicated creams, as there doesn't seem to fucking be one, I get, 'well, they're all labeled, and they're supposed to be put in baskets with which floor the resident is on, but everyone just chucks them in here. Don't worry, you'll pick it up'.

When I ask where the incontinence pads are kept for a resident, I get, 'well, they're supposed to be in the resident's room, but we normally stash a load in the bathroom downstairs. If there isn't any, just take one from someone else's room. We're waiting for another order so we're short on them at the moment'.

When I'm on the tea round making hot drinks for 40 residents and ask if there is a list of which residents have fortified drinks, or thickener agents added for ease of swallowing, I get, 'there isn't one, but don't worry, you'll get to know who has what. You'll pick it up'.

That's all very well, but it doesn't help me right now, does it?

And it doesn't help poor Gerald when I give him the wrong cup of tea without thickener in it because I don't know whether he has it or not, and he starts fucking choking on it!

Grr.

You know, I thought that working in a care home would be better for me than being in community care.

I thought, great, only one commute to one place and back. No more riding around all day getting soaked and freezing in the rain.

I thought that it would be better to actually get paid for ALL of the time spent on my shift, instead of only the time actually spent with clients.

I thought that it would be better to have a chance to get to know ALL of my clients in one place.

I thought that it would be less pressured, as there would always be another carer on hand if I needed assistance with a client.

I thought that it would be less rushed, and that it would be a more person-centred service.

I thought that it would be less stressful.

I thought wrong.

There are 40 residents here, many of them with Dementia, mental illness, and physical disabilities.

There are two televisions in the large open plan lounge areas which are constantly on, and they are on loud.

And I mean loud.

Like, all fucking day, on loud.

So loud that you want to hide in the toilet for five minutes just to enjoy the peace and quiet in there.

Only, you can't, because the 14 staff on shift, including the chefs, cleaning and laundry department, and management, plus any visitors - are only allowed to use the 1 single staff toilet, and there is always someone waiting outside.

The staff room consists of a tiny room with no door; only 1 chair in it; a fridge with a kettle on top; a coat stand; 2 rows of small lockers, and no standing room.

If you go outside in the garden to the smoking shelter, there are always a few residents out there having a fag, and only 1 staff member is allowed out at a time, so you end up cutting your five minutes of nicotine-fueled joy short to take someone to the toilet.

There is literally nowhere to hide.

Paperwork and care notes are all done on electronic Kindle-tablet thingies, but we only have 3 between us, so we fight over them to try and get paperwork done at any given opportunity when the room buzzers aren't going off, or the toilet buzzers, or nobody is asking for the toilet, and it isn't a meal time, or we aren't washing up cups and plates, or we aren't taking the menu round, or we aren't on a tea round...

There is no time to sit down and have a meal.

There is no time to get a drink.

I spent my first shift shadowing Ben, who kept disappearing. I didn't have anything to eat or drink in 12 hours, had a banging headache, and by the time my shift ended, I realised that I hadn't been to the toilet for a wee all day, but desperately needed. I had been holding it for so long, too busy rushing around to notice.

That can't be good for you.

All day long, the BLEEP BLEEP BLEEP of call buzzers from bedrooms and bathrooms go off, and if you aren't with a resident, you have to stop what you're doing and go straight away to attend.

All day long the televisions blare on while residents snooze or stare blankly at the screens in their armchairs.

All day long the SCRAPE SCRAPE SCRAPE of zimmer frames being poorly guided by confused residents along the hard wood flooring echoing in the hallways.

This is a bit intense for my liking.
What bothers me the most, is that all day long, I'm asking questions and being given vague answers which aren't really answers, just enough information to encourage me to go away from them and ask someone else.
All day long, I'm given tasks to do by the seniors in charge, but have no idea where to find anything so that I can actually do the task, then have to ask someone where to find what I'm after, then get fobbed off...
So far, I like 4 out of the 14 staff I've met. The two chefs, a cleaner, and a Senior Carer. They have actually been helpful, like when I'm hunting for a room number with no idea which of the 3 floors it is on as there is no floor plan to look at and the other carers are ignoring me and I've been up and down 2 flights of stairs already but bump into the cleaner who shows me to it; or when I have to find clean underwear and trousers for a resident who has shat themselves and there are no clean clothes in their room (which I eventually fucking found thanks to the cleaner) and I'm hunting in the laundry but nothing is fucking labeled, everyone else just already knows who wears what and I'll 'pick it up' but I haven't picked it fucking up yet because I've only been here for THREE DAYS and I've just abandoned a resident on the toilet to get the clothes but I can't find any, and everyone in the laundry department

went home like, two hours ago, and then the Senior in Charge, Lizzy, finds me stressy and tearful amongst the laundry baskets and comes to my rescue; or when I sit down to finally get some paperwork done an hour before my shift ends, because I've managed to get all my key residents on my list to bed, or ready for bed, toileted, fed and watered and comfortable, and I have NO MORE ON MY LIST! HURRAH! And so I'm midway through one resident folder on the tablet thingy, when the buzzer goes off in   bathroom 2. The other care worker, Laura, is sat opposite me doing paperwork. She has already completed 3/4 of her paperwork at lunchtime while she sent me off to get the residents all seated in the dining hall.

I look at Laura, and she looks at me. She's all like, 'oh, can you go and see who that is? I need to get this finished', and I'm like, 'I've literally just started mine, I've got loads to do still', and she's all like, 'yeah, but you need to get used to what it's like and get used to the residents, so really, you need to go…', and then the Senior, Lizzy, comes over pissed off and is all like, 'two of you are sitting here while the buzzer is going off! One of you go, I'm still giving medication!', and Laura just starts typing again, so I go, spend 10 minutes cleaning up a resident and getting her into her pijamas, taking her in the wheelchair back through to the lounge, when the buzzer in bathroom 4 starts going off. Laura doesn't even look up from her paperwork. I get my resident seated and head to bathroom 4.

Once I've sorted out *that* resident and got them seated safely in the lounge, the resident sat next to him wants to go to the toilet, so I take him, all whilst Laura sits quietly doing her paperwork.

I eventually sit back down to do mine, when Lizzy walks past, and Laura asks to go out for a cigarette. She says yes, then tells me to look after the lounge.

Of course, bathroom 3 buzzer goes off.

Come end of shift, Laura already has her coat on and walks past, and is like, 'oh, haven't you finished your paperwork yet? I've done all mine. Never mind, see you tomorrow!', and I want to lamp her.

My 12 hour shift ends and two hours later, I finish my paperwork and actually head home.

This is what I'm dealing with.

I really don't feel like I fit in here.

The kind of people I get on with and like to work with, give clear and concise instructions, tell you/show you where things are, take the time to explain things thoroughly, encourage and participate in team work, and inspire confidence.

Whereas *these* people clearly just don't want to be hassled with questions, and they are not team players.

It's really pissing me off.

AM I SUPPOSED TO JUST GAIN ALL THE INFORMATION THROUGH OSMOSIS OR SOMETHING?!

Me: Can you tell me where the toilet rolls are kept, please? I need to put one in my resident's room. They have ran out.

Staff member: They're usually kept in one of the cupboards. I'm not sure which one. I think the cleaners know, but they've gone home now *goes to walk away*
Me: So where can I get one from, for my resident?
Staff member: Erm, can't you take one from someone else's bathroom?
Me: yeah, but then they'll have no toilet paper. Isn't there a stock room or something?
Staff member: Just see if you can find one. I've gotta take my resident to bed now *walks off*
Me: *wants to scream profanities but decides not to so as not to get the sack*

Another situation example:

Me: Do you know if my resident has got any more pads anywhere in the building? There is none in her room.
Staff member: Have you looked in one of the bathrooms?
Me: Yes, but there aren't any, in any of them.
Staff member: Is there any in her room?
Me: No, I've already checked twice. She really needs some.
Staff member: I think there's some on order, she must have ran out.
Me: So is there anywhere I can get one from?
Staff member: Ooh, I don't know, maybe ask Laura? *points at Laura and walks off*
Me:*goes to Laura* Laura, do you know-
Laura: *Cutting me off, smiling and continuing to stroll past* Hi Rose!
Me: *Wants to go to the pub*

So yeah, I'm not enjoying my new work buddies.

My 2 weeks of shadow shifts are over, and I have now been officially thrown into the deep end.

I'm convinced that Laura hates me. She pretty much manages to wriggle out of doing most of her own work, but always gets her paperwork done before she leaves.

Me?

Every shift, I've ended up finishing my shift and staying afterwards for a couple hours getting my paperwork done, because it is fucking impossible to fill out all of the forms correctly during my shift, AND have a break, AND complete all of the work assigned to me.

This is my standard 12 hour shift breakdown:

8am-10am: 4-5 residents to assist getting up, washed, dressed, apply any prescribed creams, bring residents downstairs to be seated in dining hall by 10am latest as this is the cut off point for breakfast from the kitchen; take clean laundry up to their rooms and bring dirty clothes/towels back to laundry department; return any creams back to medication room; bring down any used cups, plates or cutlery from bedrooms back to the kitchen.

10am-11am: Tea round (filling kettles, tea pots, and going round with the tea trolley making drinks for 40 residents, and taking drinks to residents' rooms should they have gone back upstairs) or doing Activities (consisting of convincing old people to play cards, 4 in a row, or snakes and ladders with me to kill some time) or Washing Up (hiding in the solace of the kitchen where no residents are allowed and have a chat to the friendly chefs, washing up breakfast dishes and loading/unloading them from the steriliser) or Watching the Floor (this is basically making a futile attempt at completing some paperwork in between taking people to the toilet, trying to prevent the oldies from crashing into each other whilst they charge with their zimmer frames, convince the confused and wandering oldies to sit down to avoid having a fall, and answering the call buzzers).

11am-12.30pm: Toileting (where you try to take as many residents to the toilet as possible before lunch time to avoid them having accidents or needing to go during meal times) and Seating Residents (taking them into the dining hall, which is a job and a half because I am new here, and I don't know where people usually sit, or with who at which table, and so I'm all like, here's a space at a table, and I spend ages helping someone into the seat, only for someone else to charge at it with their zimmer frame and kick off, banging the frame on the floor and shouting 'that's my chair!' and my manager then has to help me diffuse the situation, which involves me having to re-seat a confused resident at the other end of the dining room, with other residents shouting, 'no, she normally sits next to Doris over there', pointing their shaky hands, and by the time food is ready and everyone's sat down, I want to go to the pub).

12.30pm-1.30pm: Serving Meals (you go into the kitchen, take the plates as given with names from the Chef, take the plate to the resident, and repeat, followed by stalking the dining hall looking for empty plates to take back to the kitchen, then start giving out puddings, collecting dishes as you go), Assisted Feeding (where you are assigned a resident who cannot feed themselves, and you sit next to them, loading cutlery with food, cutting it up, putting it into their mouth, holding cups up to their mouth to take a drink, as and when required), Washing up (hiding in the solace of the kitchen, same as AM wash up) and then taking residents back into lounge/rooms as and when they are ready.

1.30pm-2pm: Tea round (as above) or Toileting and Seating Residents (same as before).

2pm-4.30pm: Activities (same as before, only this time, trying to encourage residents with a bit more enthusiasm so that you can look busy and have a nice sit down with lovely Betty in the corner out of the way where staff aren't going to harass you to take on more work), 3pm Tea Round, Toileting, Care Docs (the over-complicated paperwork on those tablet thingies, in between answering those bloody buzzers), and Seating Residents (ready for their dinner at 4.30pm).

4.30pm-5.30pm: Serving Meals, 5pm Tea Round or Washing Up, then Seating Residents.

5.30pm-8pm: Bed Times (getting your assigned 4-5 residents washed and changed into nightwear to either go to bed or back in the lounge if they are staying up), Toileting, 7pm Tea Round, Watching the Floor, and Care Docs.

In between doing these tasks, we're supposed to take our breaks; go to the toilet ourselves; eat and drink ourselves; find out what dear old dazed and confused Betty had for breakfast and how much she ate so that we can type it into our tablet thingy and document it; take our Gerald to the doctors; go to the shop for Francis to pick him up some fags; answer the door and sign in visitors; convince Lorna to stop wandering about without her walking frame; stop Cynthia from flirting with Frank because he's short tempered today and wants to have his snooze in his chair in peace; guide Doris and Esther away from each other with their zimmers because they both just charge at each other and come to a halt only once they've made contact with each other and one or both of them fall to the ground; and try to stop David from wandering off because his memory loss is terrible and when he can't find the toilet, he just heads to the corner of the room he

happens to be in, or goes into the garden, whips out his willy and starts urinating.
Yep.
I swear, it's like Zimmer Frame Wars over here.
I've never witnessed anything like it in my life!

<u>Eight</u>

I start my shift at 8am.
We have the 5 minute Hand Over in the manager's office, where Lizzy, the Senior in Charge today, tells us about Cynthia's suspected urine infection and asks Laura to take a urine sample to send off for analysis, and informs us that Ethel in room 6 is now 'End of Life' care, and asks each of us to take it in turns to check on her hourly.
The rest of the information is just repeated stuff, like remembering to fortify drinks for some residents who need to put on weight, and that John in room 10, is still in hospital.
We're given our task sheets for the first half of the shift.
I decide that I'm going to be cheery and optimistic today.
Everything is going to be fine.
I have 4 to get up this morning.
OK, should be fairly simple.
I go to Maureen first, but she asks me to give her another hour.
No problem.
I go to Tom, and he says he isn't feeling well and wants to be left alone.

I tell Lizzy downstairs, who tells me that she will check on him.

I'm collecting laundry when Marge, one of the cleaners, comes over to me.

"Rose?"

"Morning, Marge!" I say, being all jolly and everything.

"Erm, have you got Mary on your list this morning?" she asks tentatively.

"Yes, why? What's up?" I ask.

"Well, she's had a bit of an accident, and... well, it's everywhere!" she says.

"OK, I'll go to her right now. Room sixteen, isn't she?" I ask, selecting the laundry basket numbered 16 and picking towels and flannels.

"Yes, sixteen. She's in a funny mood today. Saying that, she always is. OK, thanks, Rose. Give me a shout when you've done and I'll go in with the cleaning stuff," she says, hurrying off.

I head upstairs to Mary.

I knock the door of room 16, shout "Morning!", and open the door.

Wow.

I was definitely not prepared for this first thing in the morning.

Mary is pacing up and down, shuffling and muttering, trampling her tiny feet into the mess on the carpet, and she is absolutely caked in shit.

I have never seen so much faeces in my life.

"Help me!" she cries out, "you have to clean me!"

"OK, Mary, I'm coming. Let's get you in the bathroom and sort you out!" I tell her, still being cheery.

"I can't!" she says, "it's all on the floor!"

Well, Mary, you are right. It is all on the floor.

I look around the room.

The bed is absolutely spotless.

The trail of poo begins by the window, goes around in a circle in the middle of the room, then ends at the door.

Mary begins to trample her feet in it again, chanting almost, and says, "You have to get me clean! You have to clean me! You have to clean me!"

I decide that I need to take charge, here. She seems to be freaking out a little.

"Mary, take my hand," I tell her, holding out my gloved palm, "we'll get you in the bathroom, and I'll get you all cleaned up, OK?"

Mary takes my hand and I lead her into the bathroom.

I peel off her nightie whilst the shower warms up and put it into a red bag for the laundry staff, so that they'll know that it is soiled.

I clean off the more solid mess with toilet paper and flush it down the toilet, then help her into the shower.

She won't stay still. She keeps shuffling her feet and moving as I try to help her wash with a soapy flannel.

"Mary, please try and stay still for me, my love", I say calmly.

"I can't!", she says, "you're not cleaning me! You're not doing it right!"

"I'm trying to, Mary, but I need you to be still for me", I say.

She stops stomping about momentarily so that I can finish washing her bottom and legs.

"Mary, please can you sit on the shower chair? I can do your feet, then", I ask, and she does sit down, but starts tapping her feet in the shower tray.

I use a soapy flannel to scrape out the mess from between her toes.

Once she's all washed, I turn the shower off, help her to get dried, and have to dodge between piles of poo to reach her clean clothes laid out on the chair.

I help her to dress (she starts dancing around again, but I get her dressed), and then lead her into the dining hall for breakfast.

I go to find Marge.

"Hey Marge, I'm done in Mary's room now", I tell her.

"OK, thanks for letting me know. I'll get the disinfectant. Again. For the third time this week!" she says, looking annoyed.

"Does Mary have incontinence issues?" I ask, "because it doesn't say anything about it in her care plan. Maybe it needs updating".

"Oh, Rose, you have no idea!" she says, rolling her eyes, "she can get to the toilet perfectly well on her own! She does this at least once a week!"

Lizzy comes down the corridor.

"Liz!", says Marge, "tell Rose about Mary!" and heads off down the corridor.

"Of course, you don't know! You're new!" Lizzy says, looking at me.

"Don't know what?" I ask, curious now.

"Mary's family visit twice a week, and they always bring her laxative chocolate, because she says that she has trouble going to the toilet. She doesn't." says Liz.

"She doesn't? Then why-"

"With the chocolate, one or two squares a day helps to soften the stools. You aren't supposed to have more than one or two pieces a day. What Mary likes to do, is save it all up for Friday night and eat the entire bar, then she gets up every Saturday morning and shits herself!" Liz says.

"But why would she do that?" I ask, puzzled.

"She has mental health issues, basically. Her behavior gets really bad, but then she'll shit herself, get the attention she wants, and will be in a good mood for the rest of the day!"

"Right... OK..." I say, processing the information.

"Did you notice that the trail of shit in her room went nowhere near the direction of the toilet?" Liz asks, raising an eyebrow.

"I did, actually," I agree.

"That's because she jumps out of bed, shits, tramples it all in between her toes and all over the carpet, goes to the door and shouts out to anyone who walks past, 'I've shit myself', to get attention. Every week without fail. We've asked the family to stop buying it for her and told them why, but they keep bringing it in. Its a combination of that, and asking all the staff separately for a glass of prune juice. If she has more than two glasses, she shits herself." Liz says matter-of-factly.

"OK, I'll bear that in mind!" I say, and cross her off my morning duty list.

Right.
I'll go see if anyone else on my list wants to get up yet.
Hopefully no more drama.
I haven't had enough coffee yet.
And I want a bloody cigarette!

I help Maureen to get up, washed and dressed. Once I finish styling her hair and put her hearing aids in for her, she shuffles over to the wheelchair I've brought up from downstairs, sits down, and laughs at me as I try to hold the door open with one foot, pick up her zimmer frame and put it in the hall, then attempt to pull the wheelchair out backwards whilst still holding the door, as those bloody fire door closer thingies are so stiff, that the door keeps trying to slam shut, and I don't want it to catch Maureen's legs.
It's a right game, I tell you!
I have the same door issues trying to get into the hallway where the lift is, only Ben is walking past and holds it open for us.
"Thanks Ben!" I say, pulling Maureen backwards in the wheelchair.
Ben grabs the zimmer frame and places it by the lift for me.
"How are you getting on?" he asks, looking at his own duty list.
"I've still got Frank to get up. It's quarter to ten already! I don't want him to miss his breakfast!" I tell him, pressing the button for the lift, "I've asked him what he wants, so I'll have to bring it up to his room from the kitchen. And I'm supposed to have the half ten tea run. So I'm stressing a little!"

"Don't worry about the tea run, I can do that for you! I'll swap you yours for my lunchtime tea run. Does that sound fair?" he asks.

"Yes. Thank you, Ben! You're a star!" I say, steering Maureen into the lift.

"No problem! You're doing fine! Relax!" he shouts, smiling as the lift doors close behind us.

Maureen smiles at me.

"Are you OK there, Maureen?" I ask.

"Yes, dear. I'm fine. It's you I'm worried about! You need to learn to chill out!" she says.

We both burst out laughing.

"Maureen, don't you worry about me! I always get there in the end!" I tell her.

"Yes, you will, dear. You'll pick it up!" she says.

There's that phrase again.

I'm beginning to hate that phrase.

But Maureen is lovely, like so many of the residents.

I'm remembering most of their names, now, and learning which ones are the trouble makers, and which ones have fun characters. At least half of the residents have dementia so bad that they don't seem with it, or are in an almost permanent state of confusion, doped up to the eyeballs, and often sit dazed like zombies, just staring.

Maureen calls her fellow residents with dementia 'The Zombies'.

It has kind of caught on, unfortunately.

I have nicknamed them 'The Zombies' in my head now, which is awful, I know, but I feel that it is the only way I can compartmentalize my working life from my feelings.

Dementia is scary.

Dementia is fucking terrifying.

Before I got into this line of work, I had never, to my knowledge, ever met anyone with dementia.

Some clients have it, and you wouldn't know that they did. They can function independently, converse freely, make informed decisions for themselves, etc.

Some clients who have it, though, have severe memory loss and confusion, and regularly get lost on the way to the bathroom, or they are convinced that they are somewhere else, or begin to fight you as they think that you're a stranger undressing them, or that you're stopping them from going to work, or that you're lying when you remind them that they live here since their spouse passed.

Some clients get very aggressive with it, and can be violent.

Some clients don't recognise their family members who visit - even their own children - and it is absolutely heartbreaking to witness.

Some clients have had parts of their brain affected by it controlling their motor skills, and struggle with mobility, or lose control over their bladder and bowels.

There are several different types of dementia, and all of them affect the brain and body differently.

All I know, is that I have the utmost respect for anyone caring for family members or friends who have it.

I get to go home at the end of my shift, and have a break from it.

Real Carers don't.

And that is why I will never, ever judge anyone for putting their family member in a care home.

Anyway, Lizzy was listening to the radio yesterday whilst she did her paperwork. John - one of the residents - took my hand and started dancing with me around the room, smiling and laughing.

John is usually one of the 'zombies'. He rarely manages to string a coherent sentence together, and spends a lot of his day staring outside, or playing with cutlery, or wandering about aimlessly.

To see him like that - happy, dancing with those moves that he hasn't forgotten, and moved by the music - really made my day. It's nice to be reminded that my residents with bad dementia are still human beings with a history, and stories, and great dance moves, and that they are someone's child, someone's parent, that they have lived and are still very much alive underneath the 'fog' of the disease. John is a zombie who needs more music in his life to wake him up a bit.

I get Maureen settled in the dining room with her breakfast, then rush off to Frank's room with his scrambled eggs and coffee.

I finish the mad morning rush at 10.45. Today's Senior in Charge is Lynne, and I head straight for her to ask if I can go for a cigarette, am given permission, and go outside to join Maureen in the smoking shelter. I light up my glorious death stick and inhale deeply.

"You've managed to catch a break, then?" Maureen says, and chuckles to herself.
"Yes, finally!" I reply, smiling.
"You know, it's a mad house here! I'm grateful for what you carers do, but I don't think I could have done this job when I was young, all that rushing!" she says, puffing away.
"What did you do for a living when you were young?" I ask her, taking another pull from my ciggie.
"Well, I did a lot of things when I was young!" she says, "I made clothes, and I was a bloody good seamstress. Then I got married, and brought up my three daughters while my husband was away in the Army."
"That must have been tough, with your husband away," I say.
"Well, that's what we did, us women back then. We raised our kids and looked after the home. It's different now, isn't it? Most families have two working parents now, don't they?" she says, "but yes, I carried on working as a seamstress from home, making clothes for my neighbours and their friends while the girls were at school. We couldn't afford to just buy nice dresses from the shops in those days. We had to reuse fabrics from our old curtains and table cloths, can you imagine!"
"I've seen some of your clothes that you've made in the laundry. Your dresses are fabulous!" I tell her.
"They're old fashioned now, just like me!" she laughs, "but let me tell you, when I could still use my hands and sew, I could make anything! Any dress that was in a magazine or in a fashion show, I could copy, and the only

difference you'd see would be the label inside!"

"It must be great to have that kind of skill!" I say.

"Yes, it was. But now?" she holds her shaky hands up, "I can just about get a fag in my gob and a cup of tea to my lips! And that's enough for me!"

We both giggle.

I assist Maureen back inside in the wheelchair, grab a quick drink of water from my bag in the staff room, answer 5 buzzers and take 6 residents to the toilet, which takes me up to lunch time.

Once everyone has been served their pudding, I get the tea trolley out and start filling the kettles up.

Ben has very kindly already laid out the clean cups and filled up the coffee and sugar bowls, and the biscuit tin.

Simple things like that make the day go a little smoother. It is nice when people think ahead for their colleagues. I will do the same when I finish this round to make it easier for Susan, who has the next round.

These nice little thoughtful things only really stop when Laura is on shift, or Jean.

Jean isn't particularly horrible, like Laura can be. Jean is just thoughtless, I think, and only does the bare minimum that is expected of her, and not a single bit more. As soon as the shift change time comes, she's already got her coat on and is heading out the door, leaving the rest of us to finish our jobs and get ready.

She said to me on my first week, "Rose, we get paid to work our tits off for twelve hours, and write all that ridiculous crap on those tablets. There isn't time to give a damn about the rest of the bollocks. Do what you've gotta do, and sod the rest of it. Do what you get paid for. It's a job. It's work. Once shift change comes, it aint our problem anymore!". I can see where she's coming from, in a way. Yes, we do our jobs, but in this kind of work, you can't just leave things for other people to sort out. It isn't fair.

A job in Care is supposed to be conducted in a caring manner. It's such a difficult job, and there's so much to do, that a little thing like filling up the trolley with clean cups (saving a good 10 minutes of washing 40 cups and waiting for the steriliser to finish and then loading them) makes all the difference.

Jean is straight up about things, and I do respect that. I respect that it is her right as an employee to do only the tasks listed in her job description and do only what she can do in the 12 hours that she is on shift.

Laura, on the other hand, is just downright lazy, and never seems to want to be there. All of Laura's smiles with the clients are fake. She openly complains to other carers how much the residents are annoying her, in the lounge where most of the residents are sat within hearing distance.

She complains how tired she is whilst she's sat doing her paperwork and everyone else is rushing around trying to keep up with the residents' demands and way behind on theirs. But never mind.

I serve my teas and coffees, chatting away to residents, going up and down stairs to take them to people's rooms, handing them out to visitors, then collect up the empty cups, wash them, sterilise them, put them back on the trolley, fill up the bowls, and put the trolley back in its cupboard ready for later.

Lynne tells me to go out for a fag whilst it is quiet, so I do, and have a chat with Beverly, a lovely Jamaican lady, and one of the residents. I'm very fond of Bev. She always likes to sit outside after lunch to get some fresh air.

"Alright, Rosie!" she says, "come and have a seat by me!"

"Hey Bev, how are you doing?" I ask her, plonking myself down on a chair next to her, and lighting up a cigarette.

"Me? I'm alright, girl. I'm just relaxin' after me meal. What's up with your smile?" she asks.

"My smile?" I say, confused.

"Yeah, your smile! Where's it gone?" she demands.

"Sorry, I'm just tired. Here you go!" I say, and beam my biggest smile.

"Stop it!" she laughs, "them in there will think you're a serial killer with that!"

I chuckle and puff away, flicking ash into the bin.

"So what you been up to, Bev?" I ask her.

"You know me, just causin' trouble!" she laughs.

"I don't believe you, you're too nice to cause trouble!"

"Who, me? Nice?" she says, giggling.

"What have you been up to really, then?"

"Nothin' much," she sighs, "There aint nothin' to do round here. I read the paper, watch a bit of TV, read my book, try an' have a chat with them in there but they all too dazed to notice, so I come out here to enjoy the little bit of sunshine whilst it lasts. What you been up to?"
"You know me, a little bit of everything!" I say.
"Well, it's good to keep yourself busy. Keeps you out of trouble!" she says.
"Yep, that's one way to look at it."
"There aint no other way to look at it, girl. You all so busy, but you all keep it together round here, lookin' after us old fools! You work hard, earn your money, and you get your rewards in heaven for the good things you do in life!" she says, and smiles.
"Thanks, Bev. Take it easy. I'm going back in!" I tell her, stubbing out my cigarette on the bin, and head back inside.

I manage to get all of the morning shift paperwork completed by 15.30, take 7 residents to the toilet, do 4 pad changes, change 2 pairs of trousers, tell Mary for the fifth time answering her buzzer that there's no more prune juice (this is a lie, but Jo in the kitchen has told me that she's already had 2 glasses today and she's not allowed any more), then go round the building with the tea menu, taking orders for the kitchen, then help residents get settled for their evening meal. Once all the residents have had their tea and we've collected the dishes and washed up, I start taking my residents on my list into bathrooms to help them have a wash and get changed into their nightwear.

I manage to get all 4 of them ready, then sit down to fill out the paperwork.

Laura comes and sits opposite me to do hers. I say hello, but she ignores me, so I carry on typing away.

"Rose, do you know how much Catherine ate for her tea?" she asks, without looking up.

"Yeah, she had chicken sandwiches, and ate all 4 of them, and the cake." I tell her.

"OK. Do you know what Charles ate for tea?" she asks.

"I think he went with the salmon in the end. I'm not sure, though", I tell her, and continue typing.

"Did Maureen eat all of hers?" she asks.

"I don't know, Laura", I say.

"I'm just gonna put that she ate three quarters just in case", she says.

"But you don't know how much she had", I say.

"Yeah but someone would have said if she hadn't eaten anything", she says, and types away.

"Laura, do you know if Margaret had her fortified milkshakes today?" I ask her.

"Erm, I don't know", she says.

"I thought you were the one doing them today?" I say, "it was on your sheet today to make the milkshakes and take them around."

"Oh, yeah, erm, I totally forgot about them, to be honest. I had to take Nigel to the doctors so I never got round to doing them." she replies, still typing.

"OK, I'll put a no, then", I say.

"Oh, but you can just put that she had it, because they're supposed to have them twice a day", she says.
"But she hasn't had it, so I'm not gonna write that she's had it. I'm not going to lie." I say.
"It's up to you what you put," she says, "anyway, is John on your list?"
"Yeah he is, why?"
"I think he wants the toilet. He told me when I came over to you, but it just went out my head."
"Didn't you take him?" I ask.
"No, because he's not on my list", she says.
I can't tell you how pissed off I am feeling right now.
It is beyond words!
"I take plenty people to the toilet who aren't on my list, Laura, because when they gotta go, they gotta go right then! It doesn't matter about the lists!" I tell her, and get up to find John.
I am absolutely fuming.
The duty lists tell us who we have to get up in the morning, and who we have to take to bed. It tells us whose food and drink intake to monitor, and whose incontinence we need to monitor. That is it. It doesn't mean that we are only responsible for those clients on that list, as we are responsible for ALL residents in our care.
I wheel John into the bathroom and help him to get seated on the toilet.
I cannot BELIEVE that Laura would walk past someone needing assistance and just sit down, start her paperwork, and not give a shit.
Absolute bitch!

Aargh!

My eyes start tearing up a little, and I can feel my heart racing, and pressure in my head.

The stress is starting to get to me again.

Hold it together, Rose.

Breathe.

Go get the clean pijamas and the pad.

Keep your head up.

Don't lose it.

Just another 2 hours to go, and then you can go home and relax.

I spend the next 10 minutes on a hunt up and down stairs, searching for pads and John's pijamas, and eventually find some.

I have a little cry to myself in the corridor, compose myself, then head downstairs.

Once I've got John sorted and seated back in front of the rugby game on the lounge television, I pop outside for a quick ciggie with Lynne's approval.

It is now 7.10pm and Laura is sitting down next to Margaret in the lounge on a comfy chair staring at the soap opera on the TV.

I spot Lynne and head over to her.

"Everything OK, Rose?" she asks, watching Nigel swallow his tablets.

"Yeah, I just need to get my paperwork finished. I've finished everything on my list, everyone's seated watching TV and one in bed. I think Laura's finished her paperwork now. Can I please get mine done now, and have Laura watch the floor? I need to actually leave on time for once," I tell her.

"No problem, sweetheart. I'll tell Laura. Go get your work done. I'm hoping to leave on time, too, but I'm still doing meds!"

"OK, thanks Lynne!" I say, and head over to the table in the dining room where it is quiet and finish typing up my documents.

Laura seems rushed off her feet and annoyed at having to actually pull her weight for once, wheeling residents back and forth, huffing and puffing.

I take a small pleasure from this, and smile to my passive aggressive self as I finish all my paperwork at 7.50pm.

Ten minutes to go!

Yes!

Finally, I'm finishing on time!

I pop to the loo for a wee, wash my hands and splash cold water on my face, then go get bikered up with my armoured trousers, boots and jacket, pick up my bag and helmet, wave bye to everyone as I power-walk to the door and exit the building dead on 8pm.

I warm up my bike in the car park, have another cry to myself, then head off on my hour-long commute in the freezing cold rain back home.

I have 2 days off in a row, now. I've worked 48 hours this week over 4 shifts.

Next week, I've got one day on, one off, two days on, one off, then one day on and another 2 off.

I do enjoy some aspects of shift work, like having more days off in the week, and getting my paid hours done over 4 days instead of 6.

I just don't like being stuck in an overly hot building with no escape for 12 hours when I have to work with arseholes like Laura.

I also don't like that for the past 2 weeks I've gone home, drank wine and cried my eyes out over the stress of working non stop, running myself ragged once again to do the impossible job of a Care Assistant.

We are right at the bottom of the medical food chain.

We do all the stuff that nurses used to do but now don't have time for, and we get paid way less than nurses.

People always stick up for nurses, saying how overworked and underpaid they are.

I agree!

But where are all the people praising up the Healthcare Assistants?

But there you go, can't have it all.

So far I've worked here for 4 weeks.

I'm really starting to wonder if I'll be able to cope with this job.

4 fucking weeks, and I've only just found out where the staff get their coffee from, because nobody thought to tell me, or to ask me if I also wanted one when they were making drinks for everyone fucking else.

Ben has been kind to me. He's always super busy, as some of the male residents will only have a male carer see to them, and Ben is the only one who works on the day shift, but he often asks me if I need a hand, or just does little things like taking the laundry baskets downstairs when he's on his way down anyway without being asked.

There are a few really good staff here, who really care about what they do, and are helpful. But the rest just spoil it by passing everything on to someone else.

Last week, Lizzy, the senior, told me I can always ask the others for help. She found me crying in the stairwell a couple days ago.
I tried asking for help. Three times.
Each time, I was told by other staff that they would, but then they didn't because they were also too busy.
The workload is so intense here.
At least when I was doing community care, if it got too much, I could pull over at the side of the road, cry my eyes out, drink my coffee, have that 5 minutes to myself, and then carry on to my next client.
Or I could call one of my colleagues, have a good bitch to them about how shit it is, and we'd help each other out by swapping clients, or see who finished first then help the other out.
But, here?
Here I have no friends.
I do not fit in at this place.
Here, if it gets too much, I just have to deal with it and carry on rushing around, nobody to talk to or help me out, even though I help others out when I finish my morning clients first and get someone else's resident up for them.
It is only really Ben who ever helps, but he's always too busy to talk.
The managers just stay in the office all day, going back and forth from answering phones, doing paperwork, greeting visitors and going out for cigarettes every half hour.
They don't want to listen, they're too busy.
The home's Registered Manager, Vickie, saw me get tearful the once, and I went into the

bathroom to compose myself, then came out to crack on with my duties.

She called me over for a quiet word.

"Rose, I can see that you're upset, but I need you to hold in your feelings, because I can't have staff crying in front of the residents!" she said.

Which didn't help.

In fact, being told off for crying just made me cry more.

"Rose, I need you to pull it together. It's about looking after the residents. It can't be about you!" she said, "take a deep breath, then go and have a fag. Then come back and be your usual cheery self, OK?"

I could tell by the way that she said it, that this wasn't a request.

I just nodded, had a fag, composed myself, and carried on.

This is not a supportive place to work.

Everybody is in the same boat, with the same workload, but my goodness, even at my last job, the team all stuck together, and we always pulled together to get the work done, and had a laugh along the way.

Here?

Here, I'm on my own.

Everybody else has worked here for years and all know each other. They are a closed group, unwilling to accept outsiders.

And it feels really shit.

I don't think I can do it anymore.

Nine

I am going to get my shit together today, it is decided!

I pour a glass of wine, make several phone calls, and eventually get through to the Director of my last company, Phillip, who promises me that he will get my employment reference sent out to the other care firm today.

Great!

I call the care firm, speak to Marie, the administrator, who says that she's just received it, and can finally give me a start date.

Great!

I tell her that I have to give 2 weeks notice at my present job, but will be ready to start straight away after then.

Once I'm off the phone, I pour another glass, and celebrate with Pete that I'll be able to leave the care home and go back to Dom Care. After a short month of working in a home, I've come to realise that it really isn't for me. I always enjoyed the freedom that came with Dom Care, like being able to take a break when there was a gap in the rota, and being able to go home once I'd finished with my last client, even if I was early. Also just being able to have those 5 minutes to myself.

Driving around in the ice and rain is shit, yes, but being stuck in one place for 12 hours in the constant heat with non stop noise and fed up residents and being surrounded by people but feeling so alone, is, well, shitter, basically. And now I have an escape route!

Yay!

Aaand I have to write a resignation letter. Not a problem.

Hopefully it won't be too awkward.
I'm going to go with 'Family Reasons', as you never know, one day I might end up back there or with one of the staff there as my manager at another company.
I like to keep my options open, always leaving on good terms.
Great.
Party on!
Pete takes me to the pub with his friends, and we get really smashed on tequila shots.
OK, I get really smashed on tequila shots, and Pete half carries me down the road to the pizza shop on the way home.
A productive day.
I am smiling, and it feels good!
I can spend tomorrow in bed all day chilling and getting over my hangover and relax for once.
As soon as the pizza is eaten, I fall asleep as soon as my head hits the pillow.
Over and out.

It is Monday, and I arrive at work half an hour early as usual, 7.30am on the dot.
I get changed into my uniform in the staff room, put my resignation letter on Vickie's desk, check who is on staff for the next 2 weeks on the rota (Laura is on shift on all of my days on. Bollocks),make a coffee in the kitchen for myself then go out for a cigarette.
Laura comes outside to join me with a cup of tea and lights up.
"Man, I'm so tired!" she says, yawning.

"Were you on shift yesterday?" I ask, being all polite and everything, even though I want to punch her in the face every time I look at her. Well done, Rose, being all nice to the bitchy one.
Pat on the back for you.
"No, I just can't be bothered today! Were you on shift yesterday?" she asks.
"No, I had a nice day off", I tell her.
"Oh," she says, and starts typing on her phone.
And that is the end of that conversation.
Lynne and Jean come out to join us before the morning handover, and chat away.
No Vickie yet.
I feel anxious about Vickie's reaction, as she'd been talking about signing me up to do a level 3 course in Health and Social Care, paid for by them.
And now I'm leaving!
The morning handover gets done, and I ask to speak to Vickie privately.
I tell her that I need to spend time at home as my mother is unwell and working so far away from home wouldn't work in the long run.
She is very nice about it, and says it is fine, to do what I need to do, and says I'll always be welcomed back if things change in the future.
So that's that done.
I feel a little relieved, and grab my list, and crack on.
I get all of my morning clients up, washed and dressed, downstairs for breakfast by 9.50am, quickly fill in some paperwork, do my tea run at 10am, have all the cups and dishes washed up and put away by 10.40am, go for a quick

ciggie, drink some water, have a wee, take 5 residents to the toilet, fill out more paperwork, and help get everyone seated for lunch.
Jean comes over to me as we wait for the kitchen staff to give us the nod.
"You've done well this morning!" she says.
"Yeah, I'm quite pleased!" I say.
"Good. Just stick to what you've gotta do, and sod anything else! Then you can leave on time!" she says smiling, and wanders off.
The kitchen staff nod, and I go in to help serve the hot meals.
Today I assist Cyril eating his lunch, cutting up his chicken dinner and placing the fork into his mouth.
It takes about an hour for him to finish it along with his syrup sponge pudding, but I don't mind.
The others complain and try to rush him.
I allow him to take his time, and then he gets a chance to actually eat all of his food.
I'm always patient with the residents, no matter how rushed or stressed I am.
I am very bloody good at my job, and I really care a lot about what I do.
I just don't know if I'll be able to cope with it in the long run.

It is easy to see why there is a national shortage of Care Workers, as for such a demanding role - physically, mentally and emotionally - there is little reward financially. The only real reward you get is putting a smile on someone's face, and knowing that you've made a real difference to someone's day, or their life.

There is no money in this work. Most roles offer the National Minimum Wage, with between 12p and 30p per mile if out in the community.

You get no real breaks. If you actually take a lunch break, it gets docked out of your wages, plus it puts you really behind on your duties, and most of the staff end up sitting completing paperwork whilst on their breaks anyway, so what's the point in losing wages when you're working?

There are no quiet periods. Someone always needs the toilet, or feels unwell, or wants to engage in conversation, and that is my job - to assist clients to the toilet, and look after them, and chatter away should they want to - but I wish I was able to talk to someone about how I am doing, or what's on my mind, or how under pressure I feel.

And I can't.

That is why this job is a lonely job.

You spend all day looking after others, putting them first.

All your own problems and feelings have to get pushed aside.

You spend 12 hours a day with a bunch of people who have no idea who you really are, and go home.

And when you get home, the only person to offload onto is your partner, if you have one. And sometimes your partner doesn't want to talk, or listen for the fifteenth time about how much your job is killing you, because they want to relax with you after their day, and have their own stuff to talk about.

And so the arguments begin.

You're always at work.
You're always talking or thinking about work.
Why are you covering so many shifts if you can't cope with not having enough sleep?
You're always tired.
You never want to have sex anymore.
There is no real intimacy in the relationship because you're so stressed out you've shut me out.
If you find it so difficult, why don't you just quit?
Does everyone else go home crying at the end of the day, or is it just you?
You never want to do anything anymore because you're always too tired.
All you do is work, work, work!
I never see you anymore!
The most time I get to spend with you is when you're fucking ASLEEP!

And so you have a shit time at work and a shit time at home, and then you sit with your glass of wine (or cup of tea or whatever) at the end of the day, wondering why you put yourself through all of this for the sake of a job.
The job itself is more than a job, it's more of a… lifestyle.
Only people in similar roles within the Health and Social Care, or Medical industries would understand.
This is no 9-5 shit.
This is 24/7.
Nobody should ever apply for a job in Care if they think it is 'just a job'.
There are many people I've met who just wanted a job, and they didn't last long. They

soon realised that they could earn more money working in a supermarket for less hours and way less responsibility.

But this is the thing: it is incredibly easy to get a job in Care.

It is scary.

There are many people working in Care who really shouldn't be, for this reason.

You can call up a community care company, have absolutely no experience, tell them yes, you're a caring person, you get an interview that same week.

The following week you do some training to teach you about medication - you know, so that next week you can administer medication to clients who don't know what day it is -and how catheters work etc.

Then you get a practical where you play with slide sheets on the bed, and hoist each other around from chairs to beds and vice versa. And then, a few days/weeks (depending on how good the company is) of shadowing and learning how the other carers do it (which is where you learn that half the rules go out of the window and the reality of what you're really expected to do only vaguely resembles what you have learnt in training), they let you loose on your own with your own client list. BAM! You're now a Care Assistant.

It is now YOUR responsibility to hand over medication - which in the wrong dosage/combination could potentially kill - to dear old Betty who doesn't want to take it and you can't get anyone on the On-Call phone to tell you what to do. In the mean time, Betty is screaming at you that you're trying to poison her, and throws it across the room at you, and you spend the next ten minutes trying to locate all 6 of the tablets before the dog eats them.

It is now YOUR responsibility to ensure that Betty gets 3 meals a day, which are as healthy as possible. Even when she refuses to eat, and says she isn't hungry, or will only eat cakes and sandwiches (at least she's willing to eat something). YOU are now the one that gets blamed by her family that she's losing weight and isn't being looked after. It's on YOU.

It is now YOUR responsibility to make sure that Betty gets to bed on your last visit, even though she's refusing to let you put the hoist sling on her, and she won't let you put her in 'the hanging basket', as she calls the hoist, to get her into the bed. And so again, you call the On-Call phone, and they tell you to just leave her in her chair if she is refusing care. You also can't change her pad as she won't let you go near her (probably because she's missed her meds and hasn't eaten much as she's refused everything today). And so you leave a glass of water next to her with some biscuits on the table, and lock the door behind you, and go home. Only to get a phone call the next morning that the family have complained that Betty was left in her chair all night in a soiled pad, has now developed a rash (probably from the acidic urine) and isn't being looked after, and it's all YOUR fault.

It is now up to YOU to monitor Betty's behavior. You suspect that she has a urine infection, as she's been really hard to handle

the last few days, and her urine is dark and strong smelling. You report it straight away, and the District Nurse comes out five days later (they have really heavy workloads, too, and do the best they can), only to discover at this point that she now has a kidney infection due to her dehydration (you've reported for days, now, that she's now refusing fluids as well as food), and urine infection left untreated for so long, and she now has to be admitted to hospital. Even though you've done all you could do, and reported everything correctly, dealt with it all by the book, it's still on YOU as far as the family is concerned.
But YOU can't make Betty eat.
YOU can't force her to go to bed.
YOU can't touch her if she tells you not to.
YOU can't do anything more than YOU have already done.
And yet it still isn't good enough for the family.
You can't do right for wrong.
YOU did your job, and you did it well, and you did it professionally.
But you still get the blame if it all goes tits up.
Welcome to Care!

You know, if someone had asked me a year ago if I wanted to get paid £3.75 to spend 30 minutes cleaning up someone's faeces and having to deal with all of THAT, I'd probably have said no.
I'd probably have said, do I fuck!
But now?
Now I just get on with it, and it all seems normal.

Don't get me wrong, the first week out on my own, I was absolutely terrified.

I had done my training, and even ended up working as the second carer during double up calls during shadowing (I later learned that this shouldn't have happened, and was the result of under staffing, and that had anything happened, we were not insured and it would have gone to court).

I had mixed feelings about going out on my own. I didn't feel ready, but had been pressured into doing it, as my week of training and 2 days of shadowing had been unpaid, and I was anxious about paying my bills, and the company were really short staffed, so naturally I wanted to help out and earn some cash.

I got on fine with my client run. They were all clients I had visited during shadowing, so we'd already met and I had a rough idea of what I was doing.

My confidence built up and I was building good rapport with my clients who I'd see all day, every day.

It was after the first two weeks that I had more and more calls piled onto my rota, in unfamiliar areas where I'd be following a sat nav, and have pissed off clients who were expecting their regular carer, and were fed up of having to talk every new carer at each visit through their routine, and felt like they couldn't relax.

After a month, I was working in 4 different towns regularly, but different clients each shift. After 2 months, I was working mainly in Staffordshire, with clients out in the sticks, traveling down unlit and winding country lanes in the dark, where other carers were afraid to travel alone.

After 3 months, it became a novelty to have a client I was actually familiar with, and constant shift changes and rota updates became the norm.

I became so used to being under constant stress during my working day (more and more clients piled onto my ever expanding rota, ending up working 17-18 hours non stop with no break and no drink and no food) that I stopped feeling human.

I felt like I was living in a dream world, where I was only watching my life as if it were a TV show.

I felt totally disconnected from my own life.
I think that it was partly the constant lack of sleep and exhaustion which contributed to that.

It is now 5pm, and I'm collecting up the cups and plates after the residents have finished their evening meal of chicken, salad, or fish finger sandwiches with cake and crisps.

I take them into the kitchen and begin washing up, enjoying the cool breeze from the fan, and soaking in the pleasure of finally being alone in the quiet solace of the kitchen, undisturbed.

I take my time washing the dishes, and put them away once the steriliser finishes its cycle.
I want to hide in here a little longer, but Jean comes in to see if I'm finished as she wants me to help her take one of the residents to bed.

Now I have to go back out there.
Fuck.
"Hi Jean, yeah I'm finished now. Where do you want me?" I say, forcing a smile
"Follow me!" she says, and leads the way out.
I take a glance back at the kitchen as the door closes behind us.
I love that kitchen, and its air, and its silence at night.
Back into the lounge.
I fetch one of the rickety wheelchairs and open it out for the resident, James.
Jean and I both support him at the back to stand up as he takes hold of his walking frame. Jean now takes full support of him at the back as I quickly slide the chair he was sitting on out of the way, and wheel in the wheelchair behind him, locking the brakes.
"OK James, the wheelchair is behind you now, my love. Take a seat for me, please!" I say loudly and cheerily.
James is hard of hearing and does have hearing aids, but he takes them out during the day as he says that they irritate him.
Jean guides his hands to the arms of the wheelchair, and I support his back as he sits down into it.
Great. He's seated.
I push the chair out of the lounge and over to the lift, and Jean carries his walking frame.
We go up to the second floor, and Jean opens all the doors for us, and once in his room, we assist James up again, and we assist him undressing, give him a quick wash and dry, and Jean starts dressing him in his pyjamas

while I change the flannels and bundle up the laundry to take downstairs.

We help James into bed, tuck him into the covers, say goodnight, and head back downstairs.

I chuck the laundry into the baskets, then join Jean in the lounge.

It is chaos.

Olive is standing up screaming, "I want a wee! I want a wee!" at the top of her lungs, whilst Mary is trying to get access to the locked kitchen, shouting, "I need prune juice! Let me in!", tugging at the door handle.

Two buzzers are going off in the resident bedrooms, one on the ground floor, one on the second.

Sandra has sat herself on the floor and is tearing up newspapers, and Joan is wandering around without her walking frame chattering to herself.

Where do I start?

There are only 4 staff in at present: Jean, Lynne who is Senior in Charge today, Laura and myself.

"I'll sort Olive out!" Jean says, and heads over to her.

I head to Joan first, and take her her walking frame. It is fine for her to wander around and get her exercise, but she needs her frame for support. She takes it, smiles, and continues.

I then ask Mary to take a seat for me, and tell her the kitchen is locked up for the night, and that she will have to wait till morning.

She isn't happy about it, and just scowls at me, then wanders off.

Lynne comes out of the office and asks me to answer the two buzzers, then goes to try to convince Sandra to get up off of the floor.

I go to the ground floor buzzer first - to Elizabeth who wants a drink of milk bringing to her.

I tell her I will bring it to her shortly, and switch off the buzzer.

I head to the second floor buzzer - to Geoffrey who has gotten himself stuck between his chair and the bed trying to reach his remote for the television

"Have you fallen down here, Geoff?" I ask him, concerned that he may be injured.

I don't want to move him if he has had a fall.

"No, Rose, I bent over, then got down on my hands and knees to get under the bed. I got the remote but I'm stuck now!" he says and starts laughing.

"OK then, let me move the chair out for you", I say, and slide it out from beside the wall.

Geoff holds on to the bed frame, and picks himself up slowly, then sits down on the bed.

"Aah, that's better!", he says, smiling.

"Are you OK now, my love?" I say, smiling back.

"Yes, you get off, I've got everything I need now!" he says, holding the remote up.

"Alright. Goodnight, Geoff!" I say, closing the door behind me.

I rush back down two flights of stairs, fetch a glass of milk for Elizabeth, take it to her, then go back into the lounge.

It has calmed down now.

I help Lynne clean up the ripped newspapers and put them in the bin, reporting to her about Geoff getting stuck.
"Have you seen Laura?" Lynne asks me.
"No," I tell her, "I haven't seen her since tea time".
It is now 6.30pm.
One of my residents, Linda, wants to go to bed, so I walk with her slowly to the lift, and we go up to her room on the first floor.
Linda has a good sense of humour, and likes to have a bit of lighthearted banter with the staff.
I help her to undress and pull her dress over her head.
"Ooh! Buy me a drink, first!" she says, and cackles her unusual laugh.
I start to chuckle, and help her put her nightie on.
"Linda, you always cheer me up! How do you do it, staying positive all the while?" I ask her.
"Well, I don't know if you've noticed, but its fuckin' boring in 'ere, so I just brighten the place up with a bit of banter and the like, to entertain myself and keep me sane!" she laughs.
"Well, the place wouldn't be the same without you!" I tell her, as she slowly sits herself down and gets under the bed covers.
"I know that," she says, "so when I eventually die, I expect you all to have the day off and come to my funeral, and tell those leeches of my so-called family, how flippin' brilliant I was, and that they all missed out on a great fuckin' time getting to know me!"
"What?" I say, surpised.

"Look 'ere, I know I'm dying. I've had cancer on and off for years. Doc told me I've got a few months. You've been 'ere a bit now. Have you even seen one of my lot comin' to visit me?" she says.

"No, I can't say I have", I tell her.

"That's 'cause they can't be fucked to come over an' see me. I'm in a home where they put me, 'cause they dow wanna take care of me. They just want my money. And yeah, they'll get it. But I want them to know that they could've had me, and I'm flippin' priceless, I am!" she says, and giggles.

"This is a bit morbid, talking about death before you go to sleep!" I say.

"Yeah, well, you know me, I aint one for a polite topic of conversation, am I? so yeah, you lot all gotta have the day off and party at my funeral! Tell that Vickie she has to come too, and stop bein' a miserable fucker for one day to see me off!"

I start laughing.

"I think I'll let you tell her that bit, Linda! Goodnight, my love!" I say, closing the door.

"Night, Rosie!" she calls.

Linda has stage 4 ovarian cancer, and there is nothing more that can be done medically for her, except to make her comfortable.

She fought breast cancer ten years ago, having both breasts surgically removed, and then fought a cancerous brain tumor six years ago. This time she cannot fight it.

Her husband passed away five years ago after having a stroke, and then she moved into this home.

She is such a strong woman, having been through all of that, on her own, with no support from family members.

She keeps smiling, and joking and laughing, knowing that in just a few short weeks, she will get very ill as her body starts to shut down, and she will have pain, and she will die, with only the care home staff around her for comfort and to say goodbye.

Wow.

I feel my eyes start to tear up, and decide to walk the long way down the corridor to the back stairwell.

And there is Laura. She is sat on the stairs, typing on her phone.

She jumps up as she sees me.

"Hiya, I was just on my way back downstairs. I spent ages with Jack on the toilet!" she says.

"OK," I say, walking down the stairs, knowing that she was skiving, and knowing that she knows that I know she was skiving.

"How is everything in the lounge?", she asks.

"Well, it was hectic at one point, but we got it all under control."

"Oh OK, that's good then", she says, following me down.

"Oh, Lynne was asking where you were earlier, by the way", I tell her.

"Was she? When was that?"

"Maybe forty five minutes ago, something like that", I say, opening the door into the corridor, and then walk round to the lounge.

Lynne walks up to us.

"Rose, go for a fag if you want one, you haven't stopped for hours. Take a break," she says, as I nod and head to the door outside.

I hear Lynne ask Laura where she's been, and feel a little satisfaction.

This is not the kind of place where you can have a little skive without anyone noticing.

I enjoy my five minutes of nicotine outside in the cold, dark garden - a much welcomed change from the overly hot, brightly lit lounge. For once I am alone out here, and all I can hear is the road noise.

I head back in and glance at the clock.

Only forty minutes to go and I can leave. Yay!

Lynne tells me to make a drink and sit down to do my paperwork.

I do as I'm told and enjoy the rest, and also watching Laura try to multitask.

Right, back to paperwork.

Focus, Rose!

Once my forty minutes are up, I am out the door.

I smoke a quick ciggie in the car park waiting for my bike to warm up, then head home, my visor up on my helmet to let the freezing air wake me up a bit.

There is something magical about going home in the dark, when all the street lights are on, and the roads are a little quieter (well, once I'm out of the city centre, anyway!).

I get in, strip off, shower, get into my night clothes, then go to cook dinner for Pete and I. I'm tired and really cannot be bothered to cook, but Pete hasn't done any tea. He's been watching TV all day during the 14 hours I've been out the flat working and commuting, and I look round the flat and feel pissed off.

I have only one and a half hours to go before I need to go to bed, as I'm on shift tomorrow.

The laundry bag is full, so there's a good 3 loads of laundry to do, plus I will actually have to do the washing up if I want to cook anything, because all of the plates, cups, pots and pans, and cutlery are all piled up on the kitchen sides dirty (Pete has been saying for the last 3 days that he will do them), the bathroom needs cleaning, the carpets need hoovering, and he hasn't even made the bed. Damn it

"Pete, can you give me a hand in the kitchen, please?" I ask him from the living room doorway.

"Yes honey, in a minute. I'm just looking at something", he says, barely looking up from his phone.

I sigh to myself, and get cracking on the washing up. Once it is done and the dinner is simmering on the hob (I've gone with chicken curry and rice), I stick a load of laundry in the machine, quickly clean the bathroom, and I'm busy mopping when Pete comes to help.

"Oh, have you done it? Thanks honey," he says, "why don't you come and rest now before dinner's ready?"

"Pete, I've been at work all day, and yet again I've come home to a shit hole of a flat because you haven't done any housework. I'm sick of doing everything myself!" I tell him, frustrated.

"I know, and I'm sorry, I kept getting distracted because I'm so sleep deprived, I have insomnia, and I haven't had a good night's sleep in twenty years!" he says defensively.

"I know that, honey, but when I leave everything clean and tidy, and go to work all day, I come home to a pile of dishes in the kitchen that you've made, and have to clean up after you. I don't want to have to keep doing it!" I say, raising my voice a little.
"I'm off sick long term because of my illness! I'm not lazy, I'm sleep deprived!" he shouts.
"Pete, I don't want a fucking argument, I'm just saying that I don't wanna have to come home after a long day and do everything! You're telling me to come and rest!I can't rest, or relax, because my flat is a shit hole and it won't clean itself!" I shout back.
"You're the one arguing, Rose!"
"OK, whatever!" I say, finishing mopping, then I go to wash my hands and serve up dinner. I hand Pete his plate, sit down to eat mine, then say goodnight and go to bed, and sleep.

My alarm shrieks at 5am once again.
I plod along, feeling rough. My urine is dark (normal for morning) and it stings like a bitch (not normal).
Fuck, I hope it isn't another urine infection.
I keep getting dehydrated, because I just don't have enough time to get enough to drink when I'm at work.
We all rush around making sure residents get enough to drink, but there is nobody to remind us to get a drink when we're busy trying to get everything done.
I make a mental note to buy some cranberry juice on the way home.
Maybe that will help.

I stick a cereal bar in my bag, smoke a cigarette and head off.
It is raining heavily, and I've put my waterproofs on, but I can feel that I have a wet crotch.
Any fellow bikers will know that when it rains, it collects on the seat in the crotch area.
Great.
I hate having a wet bum.
Never mind.
I arrive at work at 7.32am, de-biker and put my light blue tunic on, make a quick coffee in the kitchen with a brief chat to the chef, smoke three cigarettes, have a quick stinging wee, then go into the morning handover meeting.
Afterwards, Lizzy takes me aside.
"Rose, would you like to work with me today with Ethel?" she asks.
"Yes, I can do. Let me just get my duty sheet and see who else I've got this morning," I reply.
"Don't worry about that, I've put you on the floor for this morning as we have enough staff today, so its just helping residents to the toilet and into the lounge after breakfast and stuff. Ethel is very poorly now, and we think she may pass away very soon. Have you ever worked with End of Life people before?" she says.
"Yes, I did at my last job", I tell her.
"OK, that's great. Can you meet me in room six in half an hour, then?"
"Yep, no worries. See you in a bit!" I say.
I pick up my duty sheet from the desk and look at it.

I have to escort Linda to the hospital for an appointment at 11.30am, do the 5pm tea round, and assist 4 residents into their nightwear and/or to bed, and monitor incontinence for 5 residents.

Sounds like a nice shift, to be fair.

I love escorting clients to hospital visits. You get picked up by an ambulance, have a chat for up to an hour depending on who else the ambulance has to pick up and drop off, wait for up to an hour to actually have the appointment because the clinics are always running late, then wait another hour to get picked up by the ambulance, and spend another hour getting dropped off.

It's like a nice day out for you and the resident, having a little escape from the madhouse.

I help Lorna away from the dining table and into the lounge after she's finished her cornflakes, then assist Cyril eating his porridge, putting the spoon to his mouth for him, and assist him into a chair in front of the news on television in the lounge.

I then tell Lynne I'm going to help Lizzy with Ethel.

In Ethel's room, there is a large fan on to cool the room down, as Ethel is very warm.

Her skin is hot and dry, and her breathing is loud, raspy and shallow.

She is barely conscious, and every eye movement and breath seems to be a strain for her.

We have all been checking in on her at hourly intervals, and Vickie and Sam - the managers

- have been spending most of their free time sitting with her, and talking to her.

Ethel's Nephew has been spending a lot of time with her, too, visiting daily. He is her only close relative.

Lizzy puts a cool damp flannel on Ethel's forehead and stokes her hair, speaking softly to her, and tells her that we are going to give her a quick wash and freshen up her clothes and bedding.

We undress Ethel, starting at the top half, and wash her face, hands and torso, apply barrier cream to pressure points, then help her to sit forward, wash her back, apply barrier cream, then dress her top half.

We then undress her bottom half, all the while talking her through what we are doing for reassurance, wash her groin, legs and feet, then roll her to wash her bottom and back of her legs, apply barrier cream, put a fresh incontinence pad on, then dress her.

We then roll her to one side, and I take off the old bed sheet, roll her to the other side, and Lizzy pulls the whole sheet out, folds the new one in half and places it under her, then we roll again, and I pull out the new sheet, tuck it in and place the slide sheet under her.

One more roll, and Lizzy pulls the slide sheet out, and we lay Ethel on her back, and slide her up the bed, put fresh pillows under her head, and tuck her in with fresh blankets.

Lizzy combs Ethel's hair, and I take out the laundry and dispose of the old pad.

Just four weeks ago, Ethel was pacing up and down the lounge and hall ways, causing havoc and walking off with other residents' drinks and snacks, wandering into other people's rooms, rarely staying still for long.

Then one day, she wouldn't get out of bed, and the doctor was called.

And just like that, she was dying.

I find it strange that I was chasing her around the lounge just four weeks ago, trying to give her her sandwich, and walking round the room holding hands to guide her to the little snug at the back, to hold the baby doll.

She absolutely loved that doll and would cradle it in her arms for hours, then put it into its Moses basket, saying, "shh, shh", and sit for a while watching over it.

Lynne tells me to go for a fag whilst its quiet, so I do, taking George out with me in his wheelchair.

George always makes me laugh, because whenever he sees me making a beeline for that door into the garden, he waves at me and mouths 'please', so I always take him, and he always asks me about the Blues score, and I keep telling him that I don't watch the football, and he keeps telling me that I don't know what I'm missing.

After our ciggie, I take George to the toilet and change his pad, then take Mary some prune juice (once I check with the kitchen staff that she hasn't already had some today). Then I go to get Linda's coat and scarf from her room for her, and we wait for the ambulance driver to arrive to take us to the hospital for her appointment.

The driver, Jim, arrives, and we head outside into the cold February air, and get into the ambulance.

"Alright ladies, get your seat belts on! We're going for a ride!" he says loudly from the driver's seat in his broad Black Country accent. I've met Jim before, escorting other residents to appointments. He's one of those people who always puts a smile on your face with his cheeky banter and chit chat, and he just really likes his job.

I wonder what that's like.

I help Linda get her seat belt clipped in, clip on my own, and we set off into busy Birmingham traffic.

"Ladies, did I ever tell you that I used to be a lorry driver?" Jim shouts from the front.

"Yes!" Linda and I call out in unison, and we both laugh.

"That's right!", he shouts, "but did I ever tell you both how lovely it is to be driving around all day with the lovely company of your lovely selves, not being all lonely in my truck without you?"

"Jim, I've told you before, I'm old enough to be your mother, and this one," she says, pointing at me, "is young enough to be your daughter, so don't even go there!" Linda shouts to Jim.

"Now, now, my lady! Age is just a number!" Jim says, jokingly.

"Well at my age, I know better than to be chatting up people in the back of an ambulance!" Linda says, laughing.

"Alright, alright, I get the point!" Jim says, "can't blame me for trying! So what time's your appointment, then?"

"It's at half twelve. Don't they bloody tell you that on the phone?" Linda calls.

"No, my lady, I just get told where to go and when. No one tells me nuffink!"

"Well, they ought to sort that out, Jim! No good, that! Anyway, you just focus on gettin' me to where I've gotta go!" Linda shouts, smiling.

"Alright, alright, keep your hair on!" Jim laughs.

I am so glad that I've got this on my duty list today. Linda is lovely, and Jim is funny. It's so nice to get out for a little while.

On route to the Queen Elizabeth Hospital, we pick up another lady from another care home with her carer, and we all have a good chat. Linda asks the other client what the food is like at their home, and me and the other carer briefly discuss how good it is to escape our respective homes for a few hours.

Jim drops the others off at their department first, then drops Linda and I at ours.

"Now, don't forget to give me a ring when you're all done, ladies, and I'll come and rescue you both from the scary hospital, bein' all fearless and handsome an' that, and I'll give you both another ride! Unless Leroy beats me to it, that is!", Jim says.

"Is Leroy good looking?", Linda asks.

"No! He's an' ugly sod, is Leroy!" Jim says laughing, "just kiddin'! He's a good lookin' lad, all dark an' handsome, tall, well built an' the like, but he don't talk much, so you won't get all the fun you get with me!"

"I suppose we'll give him a chance, if he comes instead!" Linda says.

"Now, now, my lady! No need for that! You'll miss me really!", Jim says, "anyway, I've gotta go, and so have you pair! Ta ra a bit!"

"See you later, Jim!" I shout as he gets back in his ambulance.

Linda giggles as we walk into the reception, stops, and says, "shall we go to the pub instead? These lot are only gonna tell me what I already know, that I'm dying. Can we not just go and have a few bevvies?"

I must admit that I am tempted at this point. I always bring my phone and purse out with me when escorting clients, as if we are here for a long time, I may need to purchase food for a diabetic client, or call for help.

I could go to the pub with Linda, but it would be extremely unprofessional, even if she is dying, because I am responsible for her in my care.

"I want to say yes, but its a no, Linda, sorry! I'll get the sack!" I tell her.

"Rose, I am disappointed in you!" she says, seriously.

"I have to be professional!" I tell her, and she bursts out laughing.

"Fuckin' hell, Rose, lighten up! Let's get this over with, shall we?!" she says, and walks up to the queue ahead of me.

We wait 45 minutes to be seen, and at the appointment, the oncologist tells Linda that he's reviewed her latest scans from last week, and that she may only have between six and twelve weeks to live.

I sit there next to her as she takes it in, and then she grabs my hand.

I hold it, and listen as the oncologist explains that the cancer has spread rapidly, and from what he says, it has pretty much spread over most of her organs.

"Fuckin' hell", Linda says to the doctor, "I'm actually goin' to die pretty soon, then, aren't I?"

"Yes, I am sorry", the doctor says.

We leave the clinic, and Linda wants to go to the toilet. We both go in, and I use one whilst we're in there.

"Rose, I'm gonna fuckin' die. I'm actually gonna fuckin' die!" she says as we are washing our hands, and her eyes begin to tear up.

"Linda, I'm sorry. I don't know what to say!" I tell her softly, and dry my hands, trying to hide my own teary eyes.

"There's nothin' you can say, love, its just hit me harder than I thought it would!" she says.

"It's pretty shit, then," I say.

"That's the first time I've ever heard you swear, our Rose!" Linda laughs.

"Well, it seemed appropriate!" I say, and smile.

"I guess it is! So, you comin' to the pub or what? That ambulance bloke ain't gonna be here for an hour and a half, the receptionist said. We've got time!" she says.

"Linda, I'm not drinking! I'll have a coffee or something." I tell her.

"Well, I might be dying, but I still ain't sad enough to drink on my own, so I guess its a fuckin' coffee in the hospital cafe then, you boring cow!" she says, and I burst into laughter.

"I think I can manage that!" I say, and we walk up to the cafe for a coffee and cake.

"You know, I spent years not eatin' cake to keep healthy and have a nice figure. What a fuckin' waste of time!" Linda says through a mouthful of cake, "'cause I went an' got frickin' cancer anyway!"

"Yeah, but you never know what's around the corner, do you? If you'd known, would you have eaten loads of cake and gotten really fat instead?" I ask.

She looks thoughtful for a moment, and says, "well, no, I guess not. But it pisses me off to know how much I denied myself! I didn't drink much, or eat too much, an' I exercised, an' I didn't smoke, because I wanted to be healthy! What a load of bollocks!"

"Well, my dad was a marathon runner, ate the best of everything, really looked after himself, and he died of a brain tumor aged fifty five. But I don't think that he'd have done anything differently if he'd known, because he really loved life up until he passed away", I tell her.

"How old were you when he died?" she asks.

"I was seventeen," I reply.

"That must have been tough on you", she says.

"Well, I knew that he had cancer, and that he was going to die, but it didn't actually make it any easier when he did. I thought it would, but when he went, it still came as a complete shock. Nothing prepares you for losing a parent", I tell her.

"I remember when my parents died. They were old, in their eighties, and I was in my fifties. You're right, even when you know, you ain't prepared."

We sip our coffee in silence for a little while.

"Rose, shall we go back to reception an' wait for our Jimmy? Or Leroy?" Linda asks.

"Yeah, sounds like a good idea!" I say, and put our rubbish in the bin, and head back down to reception.

Linda and I pass the time looking at funny videos of cats on the internet on my phone, before our transport arrives.

"Well, well, well! If it isn't the two most fabulous ladies in the Midlands!" Jim says loudly, walking over to us, "you're both in luck, you've got me again!"

"Oh no, not you again!" Linda says, laughing.

"Oh, yes!" Jim says, "come along, ladies!"

We get into his ambulance and head back to the care home, after dropping off a gentleman on route.

When we get back, it is almost 4 o'clock. I warm up Linda's lunch for her - a beef dinner - and serve it to her, then go into the office to speak to Lynne and Vickie, to tell them what was said in the appointment.

"She's walking around, being her lively self - you wouldn't think that she's got less than three months to live! The poor woman!" Vickie says, "we'll have to keep an eye on her, try and keep her spirits up!"

"You often find that people with a degenerative illness will be fine one minute, and then the next, become really ill. It can happen very suddenly, like with Ethel. We all need to keep an eye on her. I'll put it in the handover notes", Lynne says.

"OK. I just want to mention that Linda asked me to go to the pub with her for a drink after her appointment. I said no, obviously, but I think it might be nice if someone could go out with her one afternoon maybe, while she's still well enough to go and enjoy herself," I say.

"Yes, we can arrange that, Rose. A dying woman can have whatever she wants! I'll see to it that it happens," Vickie says, "now go have a fag and a coffee before tea time!"

I do as I'm told.

I puff away quickly, down my coffee, and go back inside.

I take 3 residents to the toilet, change 2 incontinence pads, then help serve the teatime sandwiches to the residents, running back and forth up and down stairs with plates and hot drinks to those staying in their bedrooms, then do the tea run.

Once I've collected and washed up the cups and plates, put them in the steriliser and put them away, I sit down to start my paperwork. Laura is sat doing hers opposite me.

Joan charges around the room with her zimmer frame, making that awful scraping noise. I have previously tried to explain to her how to lift the back of it, push it forward, put it down, step into it - but she seems to prefer to just charge with it instead, wearing out the ferrules.

I have written a list of what my residents have had for their lunches and teas, and Lynne has told me how much everyone has had, and who had their fortified milkshakes, and Jean has told me who on my list has been to the toilet etc.

I type quickly, then go to start getting my residents ready for bed.

I check in on Ethel, and Lizzy is sat with her, stroking her hair and placing cool flannels on her forehead.

"Hi Rose, she's alright. She hasn't been awake since this morning. I think she may pass away soon," Lizzy tells me quietly.

I take Ethel's hand in mine and stroke it.

She is still very warm and her skin is still dry. I notice that the skin on her arms is looking quite thin, and she has an intravenous drip attached to her.

"Is her skin breaking down, now?" I ask Liz quietly.

"Yes, her body is starting to shut down now," she says, and points to the drip, "the District Nurses came this afternoon and put that in. It is a Morphine drip, to help soothe her and give her pain relief. It's unlikely that she'll regain consciousness now".

"Oh, OK. I'm glad she's not in pain." I say.

"Me too. I'm OK here, Rose, I'm gonna sit with her for a while, so you can go and do your paperwork if you like", Lizzy says.

"OK, I'll leave you to it. Night, Ethel," I say, and leave the room quietly.

I take 2 residents to the toilet, then go finish my paperwork.

I manage to complete it 10 minutes before the end of shift, and decide to go and have a chat with Cyril for 10 minutes.

Sam, the Deputy Manager, comes over to us and sits down.

"Hi Cyril!" she says, cheerily.
Cyril nods at her, and then Sam turns to me.
"Are you able to work tomorrow, Rose? We're gonna be short staffed as two have phoned in sick with a stomach bug. I've only got Jenny and Ben in, and Lizzy will be in charge tomorrow doing medication, so I need two more. I've asked Laura and she's agreed to do an early for me, eight till two. Could you please do eight till eight?" she asks.
I think about it for a while, then say, "I can do a late, two till eight, if that's any good? I've got a couple errands to run in the morning".
"That'll be great, Rose. We can just about manage with three carers. I'll be around anyway, so I can always help out. Thanks for that!" she says, getting up.
"You're here late, Sam!" I say.
"Yes, well I've been filling out loads of paperwork that needed done by today, so I'm going home now! You should get off, too, its almost eight!" she says, and walks off.
I look at the clock and get up.
"Night, Cyril!" I say to him, but he's nodded off.
I wave to the night staff who are just starting shift, go to the staff room, biker up, and I'm out the door just after 8pm.

I arrive home at 21.07. Pete waves to me through the living room window as I park my bike up outside. He is sat watching TV.
I walk in, taking my jacket off and putting my helmet down.
"Hey honey!" Pete calls, coming into the hall to hug me and kiss me.

"Hey Pete. What's for tea, then?" I ask, smiling as I kick off my boots and take my protective trousers off.

"Well," he says, "I can make beans on toast if you want?"

"OK, that'll do, thanks," I tell him, heading into the bathroom to undress and switch the shower on.

"You're off tomorrow aren't you?" he asks from the doorway.

"I told Sam I'd cover tomorrow, but I'm only doing two till eight, because I need a lie in and have to drop some paperwork off at my new job's office in the morning", I tell him.

"Oh, OK then," he says, looking disappointed.

"What's the matter, honey?" I ask him, getting into the shower.

"Nothing, I just thought it might be nice to spend some time together, that's all," he says.

"I've got Thursday off, so we can spend that together if you like?" I say, washing my hair.

"OK, yes, that'll be nice. I'll go and make us beans on toast then. It'll be ready in fifteen minutes," he says.

Once showered, I dry off, put my night clothes on, and go into the kitchen to help Pete serve up.

We sit down to watch a film together, but he falls asleep halfway through, and I turn it off, go for a cigarette outside, then wake him to take him to bed.

I then go and hang up the wet laundry that has been sitting in the basket since I did it last night, wash the dishes, clean off the kitchen sides, and go to bed myself.

I have decided to try to keep on top of the housework, seeing as Pete isn't doing it.
I know that he is tired all the time and gets distracted, but when he is in my flat all day using the plates and cutlery and not cleaning up after himself, and doesn't put the washing machine on or hang the laundry up, I get really annoyed at having to come home from work tired and wanting to wind down and having to do everything, when he has been watching TV all day or lying in bed looking on the internet, relaxing and snoozing or whatever.
I get frustrated with him, and we argue a lot about it.
He gets annoyed with me because he thinks I don't understand his illness, and I get annoyed with him because I just want him to understand how hard it is to relax when I come home to a shit hole everyday and have to do everything.
He gets annoyed with me because I spend a lot of time at work, or being upset over how tired and drained I am because of work and never want to do anything, and I get annoyed with him because I don't want to do anything other than relax at home and play catch up with the housework when I'm not at work, and don't have the energy to go out places, and have to explain to him yet again that if I didn't have to do all the housework on my days off, that I would have time and energy to do things.
But there you go.
I lie awake for about an hour, thinking about things, like how disconnected I feel from my

own life, and hoping that when I start my new job in a couple of weeks, things will settle down and I'll feel happy again.

I love the work I do, and my clients are great. I had a bad experience with my old company, and I don't like working in this care home. This next company, I hope, will be much better.

Ten

This morning, I get up with ease for a change. It is nice to have enough time to wake up and have a coffee or two before setting out, which is why I have put my availability down for working afternoons and nights at my new job. This way, I will still have time to go to appointments or go shopping or whatever during the morning before I have to go to work.

Plus, the morning shift is always the hardest, as it is a rush getting clients up, washed and dressed. Putting them to bed is usually easier. I will be working on a Sunday for a full 16 hour day, but as I won't start on Monday until 3pm, I will have enough time to get to sleep and wind down after my shift.

I have learned that to work in a stressy and difficult job, it is important to have enough time to relax and sleep and have a life outside of work.

I pop into the office and drop off my signed paperwork, and agree to meet with the Coordinator in a week's time to sort out my shadow shifts.

I then pop home for some lunch, have a brief chat with Pete, and go out to work.
It takes longer to get there in the afternoon through the busy city traffic, but I arrive 20 minutes early, so I grab a coffee and smoke 2 cigarettes before I start my shift.
I pick up my busy duty sheet from the desk as Laura walks past in her coat to leave and blanks me as I call 'hello'.
Ben and Jenny are sat doing their paperwork from this morning, so I watch the floor, and take 6 residents to the toilet, change 1 set of trousers, change 5 incontinence pads, and do the 3pm tea round and wash up, stacking the trolley with clean cups, and filling up the sugar and coffee bowls ready for the next lot.
Then I help Jenny to get the tea time orders ready for the residents and serve up.
Ben appears, slightly out of breath and looking very tired.
"I've just been searching everywhere for a pair of trousers for Charles!" he says, grabbing a quick glass of water.
"Did you find some?" I ask him, taking the last plate out of the kitchen to the table for Joan.
"Yes, eventually! I've got the tea round to do now, and I've still got loads to do, and paperwork!" he says, following me back into the kitchen to fill up the kettles.
"Do you want me to do your tea round, Ben?", I ask him.
"Please, if you wouldn't mind!" he says.
I take the kettle from his hands.
"No problem. Go do what you've gotta do!" I tell him, and take over the teas.

"That's nice of you to do that, Rose!", Jenny says to me, putting some dishes in the sink.
"Yes, well we're a team, we have to help each other," I say, "anyway, I'm only on half a day today, so I'm not as tired as you guys!"
"That's true. I just wish everyone who worked here would be like that!" Jenny says, "it would be a much nicer job if they were!"
"See you in a bit!" I say, and head out to serve the drinks.

Yes, it would be a nicer job if everyone chipped in and helped each other, but unfortunately, not everyone does. I've found that the more a person does, the more is expected of them, so I get why Jean does only the bare minimum, and I get why Lynne focuses on only her role of doing medication and charts for the day so that she can leave as soon as shift change comes.

Bloody hell, I mean, I want to leave as soon as shift change comes! Don't we all!

But people, like Ben, for example, rush around trying to do everything plus trying to help everyone else, and then it becomes expected, and taken for granted.

When Ben has a day off, everything goes to shit around here, because he's been running round doing everything for the last 12 years, and just does what needs to be done without being asked.

He's lovely and kind, and I watch some of the other staff take advantage of that.

I finish the tea round, wash up in the kitchen, load the trolley, help 6 residents get into their nightwear, take 3 to the toilet, then come end of shift, I sit down to finish my paperwork.

Ben walks past and asks me how much I have left to do.

"Just 4 residents now", I tell him.

He grabs one of the tablets and sits down with me.

"I'll do Maureen and Charles", he says, and starts typing.

"Thanks Ben, I appreciate that!" I say.

Ten minutes later, we're both done, and I get kitted up, and head home.

I get in at 21.27. Pete comes out to me as I lock my bike and light a cigarette.

"You're late. Was traffic bad?" he asks.

"No, I just had to finish my paperwork. We were short staffed, so we were busy." I tell him.

"You shouldn't be staying late unpaid, Rose!" he says, "why do you keep doing it?"

"I'll get in trouble if my paperwork isn't done, honey. I've already spoken to Sam about it. I told her that I'd been staying behind after shift for an hour just doing paperwork almost everyday, and that I wanted paid overtime, but she said that Mark, the boss, won't pay it and says it is possible to do it all whilst on shift-"

He cuts me off and says, "but it isn't! You hardly ever finish on time! You shouldn't work for free, just leave when your shift ends, if it isn't done, its their problem!"

"It isn't that simple, Pete-"

He cuts me off again, saying, "yes it is! It is very simple, in fact! Just don't do it!"

I sigh and finish my cigarette.

"Rose, don't you agree? Don't you agree how simple it is to just walk out when your shift ends?" Pete says.

"I hear you, Pete. Yes it is simple. But the consequences aren't. Anyway, just a week to go!" I tell him.

"OK, you're welcome!" he says sarcastically, "I'm just being supportive. I wish you'd appreciate that!", he says, and goes inside.

I remain silent, as it seems like he's pushing for an argument. I put my cigarette out, and follow him in.

I wake up Thursday morning to Pete handing me a coffee and telling me that he wants us to go on his bike for a ride out somewhere.

I agree and tell him I'm not fussed where we go, that he can choose.

"I want you to decide where we go, Rose!" he says.

Now, I've been awake for less than 15 minutes, and I could not care less where we go. I don't want to do anything today, but I told him we'd spend some time together, and he rarely leaves the flat unless I go with him these days, so I have agreed to go outside.

"How about Bridgnorth?" I suggest.

"I was thinking further than that, really. Where else would you like to go?" he replies.

"I would like to go to Bridgnorth, and have a coffee and a walk down the river. If you want to go further, maybe you should pick somewhere?" I tell him.

"I don't want an argument, Rose!" he says, raising his voice, "I just want to do something nice for us!"

"What the fuck, I'm not arguing with you! You asked me to pick somewhere, and I have!" I complain, sipping my coffee, "where do you want to go, if not Bridgnorth?"
Pete sighs and walks out of the room.
I sip my coffee, feeling irritated.
What did I do to piss him off?
Fuck knows.
He comes back with more coffee for himself.
"Have you though about where else you'd like to go?" he asks.
"No I haven't, Pete. I've just woken up, and like I said, I fancy going for a walk down the river", I tell him calmly.
"I want to go for a long ride, though," he says, "somewhere further".
"Well, where were you thinking?" I ask.
"I don't know, I wanted you to decide!" he says, sounding frustrated.
"How about somewhere in Wales?" I suggest.
"No, because I haven't got enough petrol", he says.
We sip our coffee in silence for a while.
"OK," he sighs, "we'll go to Bridgnorth".
"Alright then", I say, and get up to get dressed.

We have a nice day in Bridgnorth, having coffee and cake in a cafe, and walking by the river in the winter sunshine holding hands.
We get back in the evening, and have fish and chips from the local chip shop, and then shower and get ready for bed.
I hang up my damp uniform, hoping that it will be dry by the morning, and climb into bed.

I get to work early, have a coffee and smoke three cigarettes outside.

Laura pretty much ignores me, and types away on her phone.

Lynne comes outside for a cigarette with Lizzy, and Sam joins us.

We all go in for the morning handover meeting. Afterwards, I pick up my duty sheet to see who I have this morning to get up.

I go to Mary first, who is dancing all round the room trampling her shit into the carpet. I have a right game trying to get her into the bathroom to get her cleaned up. I get her sorted with her refusing to let me put her medicated cream on her knees once she's washed and getting dressed.

I say its fine, and she just looks at me confused.

"Do you want your cream on, Mary?" I ask her.

"No! You're not putting that stuff on me!" she shouts.

"OK, I won't." I tell her, and proceed to roll down her trouser legs and put her slippers on for her.

She seems disappointed that I'm not playing along with her. I'm just not in the mood for playing her games today.

I ask her to come with me into the dining room for breakfast.

"I don't want to go in there!" she shouts, folding her arms.

"OK, I'll bring your breakfast to you in here. What would you like, Mary?" I ask her calmly.

"You can't leave me in here! It stinks like shit! There's shit everywhere!" she shouts.

"Then come with me into the dining room", I say.

She looks annoyed, but shuffles over to the door with me, and takes my hand to walk with her to the dining hall.

I get her seated and give the kitchen staff her order. I then let the cleaners know about the mess in her room, and bring the soiled laundry in a red bag to the laundry staff and inform them.

Next is Gerald, who won't let me touch him and refuses to get up.

I tell Lynne, who comes with me back to his room to try and find out what the matter is, and give him his medication.

Gerald still will not let either of us touch him. He takes his tablets with a glass of water, but says that he wants to be left alone and isn't getting up today.

Lynne tells me to try him again later on.

I go to Linda to help her get up. She's already midway through her wash, so I help her wash and dry her back, get dressed, and then walk with her to the dining room.

David sings Frank Sinatra songs to me whilst I help him shower and get dressed, then I bring him down in his wheelchair to the breakfast table.

Laura comes up to me.

"I've just been upstairs to Joyce because she was buzzing. She's on the toilet and said she's ready to get up now," she tells me, and goes to sit down to do her paperwork.

"OK, I'll go there next", I tell her.

I pop up to Joyce, who has started buzzing again. She wants some help getting off of the toilet. I help her, clean her up and assist her with her wash.

There are two soiled incontinence pads on the floor by her bed. I bag them up to dispose of on the way out.

Laura would have seen those as she came in. She just left them.

I help Joyce get dressed and take her down for breakfast, stopping off at the shower room to dispose of the soiled pads in the yellow 'infectious waste' bin.

Any other member of staff would have bagged them up and disposed of them, but not Laura.

Gerald is still refusing to get up, so I bring him up his full English breakfast that he asked for, and pop it on his trolley with a mug of tea.

I go out for a quick cigarette, then take 4 residents to the toilet.

I get back, and quickly sit down to start my paperwork before lunch time.

Laura comes over to me and sits down to do more paperwork.

"Rose, Cynthia wants the toilet. She's on your list." she says, typing away.

"Why didn't you take her?" I ask calmly.

"She's not on my list, she's on yours and I have paperwork to do," she says, not looking up.

"Really? So you've refused to provide care to a resident because you have paperwork? Wow!" I say irritated, and get up.

"I haven't refused care, she's not on my list!" she argues, finally making eye contact.

I want to swing for her!

Lynne comes over, and says, "what's the problem, girls?"

"Laura has just sat down and told me that Cynthia needs the toilet, and she's walked right past her and come all the way over here to do her paperwork, because she's not on her list!" I tell her.

"It doesn't matter whose list she's on, if a resident needs assistance, you assist them!" Lynne says sternly, "Rose, you go and see to her. Laura, a word!"

I go and take Cynthia to the toilet, feeling pissed off, but I'm all smiles and kind towards my client, being patient with her, fetching her clean underwear and a clean skirt to put on, as she had been incontinent. Probably because she had to wait for assistance

Once Cynthia is seated comfortably in the lounge with her magazine, I go to the staff room to have a sip of water, and cry to myself. I'm so fed up.

I want to give Laura a good slap. She talks to me like crap and is so unhelpful! I hate working with people like that!

I grab my phone out of my bag and text Pete, asking him to call the home, saying there's a family emergency so that I can go home.

It is only 11.30, and I simply cannot stay here all day having to work alongside that lazy, selfish bitch!

I am in tears already.

I am so stressed out.

I just want to go home.

I compose myself, and sit down to do some paperwork quickly. Lynne has sent Laura to do the running around answering buzzers and taking residents to the toilet.

Half an hour later, Lynne tells me that there's a phone call for me. I answer it, and Pete, bless him, tells me that there's an emergency and I need to come right away.
Lynne nods to me and says, "go, Rose, we'll cover your shift!".
I get my things from the staff room and head off home.
I pull over on route to cry and have a cigarette, then continue.
I have decided that today is my last day.
I only have three shifts left, and I decide to call tomorrow to tell Vickie or Sam that I won't be able to do them due to family stuff.
In reality, it is for my own sanity.
I need to sort my shit out and start my new job fresh and ready. I won't be able to cope, having to put up with Laura for 12 hours each day, and all the rushing.
I have been crying almost every day, which is not healthy.
Plus I need to go to the doctors to get treatment for my urine infection that has worsened. I'm now getting abdominal pains and it feels like I am weeing glass.
I get home, strip off, and put my night clothes on.
Pete makes me a coffee and gives me a shoulder rub.
I tell him that I'm not going back, and he agrees that it is wise.
We have takeout pizza and watch a comedy film before we fall asleep.

The next week is spent going to the doctors and being put on a 3 day course of antibiotics for my urine infection, drinking lots of cranberry juice, drinking lots of wine, making love, watching TV, going for bike rides, and relaxing.

On Monday, I meet with Paula, the Care Coordinator at my new place.
"Right, Rose, I've put you on shift with Suki tomorrow night, then with Jaspreet on Thursday, and Kelly on Sunday mornings and lunches, then Lydia Sunday teas and bedtimes", Paula says, stapling the rotas she has just printed off together.
"No work tonight or Wednesday?" I ask her.
I had been promised at least 44 hours a week at interview.
"No, things are a bit slow in the areas local to you at the moment. The rotas used to be rammed, but a lot of clients have passed away, so we're just waiting for things to pick up and trying to get new clients", she says.
"OK. What about the other areas? I'm willing to work all over Wolverhampton. I don't mind what area, as long as I'm kept in the same area the entire shift", I say.
"OK, well I can put you shadowing in Wednesfield and Low Hill next week if you like, and Pendeford and Oxley?" she says.
"Yes, that would be great, thanks", I say.
"OK, well I'll sort that out for you", she says, and hands me two boxes of gloves and two packs of disposable aprons, "if you pop back in on Monday, I'll give you the rotas for next week. Make sure the girls fill out your shadowing paperwork, and don't forget to do your time sheets and hand them in by

Wednesday each week,or you won't get paid", she says.
"OK, see you next week!" I say, and head outside to where Pete is waiting for me.
We go for coffee and I tell him about the shifts for this week.
"Great, you can spend more time with me!" he says.
"Yes, I can, but that means I'll only be working twenty five hours this week, instead of forty!" I tell him, "so I'm not gonna have a lot of money! Plus, i have to work two weeks in hand before I get the first week's pay, which will be shit!"
"Oh, I never thought of that," he says.
"So things will be extremely tight for the next month or so!" I say.
"Don't worry, Rose, It'll work out OK! I'm sure you're gonna love your new job!" he says and kisses me.
I hope so.
I really hope so.

It is Tuesday, and I am ready to start my first shadow shift. I'm meeting Suki outside a client's house at 15.20. It had said 14.40 on the rota, but Suki said on the phone that this was the best time.
I have a quick cigarette, pop a mint into my mouth, stick my waterproof sat nav into its holder on my handlebars, and head off to the first client.
I arrive in 11 minutes. It is strange to be working so close to home. This week, I will be working in the Penn and Merry Hill area of Wolverhampton.

Suki arrives five minutes behind me, in her car, followed by the double up carer, Melissa.
"Call me Mel," Melissa says, shaking my hand.
"OK Mel. I'm Rose," I say, then I turn to Suki, "hi Suki!"
"Hiya, you alright? Have you done Care before?" she asks me.
"Yes I have", I reply.
"You'll be fine then! Let's go in and I'll introduce you to Mrs Patel!" she says, and walks up the drive to the front door.
A tall Asian lady answers the door and lets us in.
"Hello Aunty!" Suki says to her, "we've got a new lady with us today. This is Rose!" she points to me.
"Hello!" I say, and she smiles and shows us through.
Suki and Mel both use the phone to log in, and then we go into the back room to see Mrs Patel.
"Hello Aunty!" Suki calls to Mrs Patel, "we've come to see you and get you sorted out. We have a new lady, Rose with us!" she says, as we all put our gloves and aprons on.
Mrs Patel stares at us, and makes a crying noise.
An Asian music channel is on in the background on the television, with colourfully dressed dancers singing and dancing.
"Aunty is bed bound now, and she has dementia. What we do in this call is we change her pad if it needs changing, put barrier cream on as she has pressure sores, change her into her night clothes and turn her. She gets turned at every call, and the family

does it as well. They give her her meals. We always try and encourage her to drink when we're here, too." Suki tells me, as she and Mel take the brakes off of the bed and pull it out from the wall so that Mel can get round the other side.

"Have you seen pressure sores before?" Mel asks me.

"Yes, I've had clients who have had them in the past", I reply.

Suki speaks to Mrs Patel in Punjabi, and then she and Mel pull the covers off of her, and Suki puts the slide sheet under her, and then they roll her to the other side, and Mel pulls the slide sheet out.

Mrs Patel cries out.

"She's in pain, but she also screams a lot when people go near to her, or try and take her covers off. She can understand English, but with her dementia, she can't speak it back anymore. We talk to her in Punjabi because it seems to calm her down when she's upset, maybe because its more familiar to her", Suki explains.

Mrs Patel cries out again when Mel pulls her trousers and pants down and takes out her incontinence pad.

"Its OK, Aunty, I'm just changing your pad," Mel tells her, "gonna get you cleaned up!"

Mel uses tissue and baby wipes to clean Mrs Patel's bottom, applies barrier cream to her red sores, and puts the new pad in place, then puts her clean underwear and pyjama bottoms on, being careful not to knock the catheter pipe.

Mel uses the bed remote to put her in a sitting position, and Suki helps support Mrs Patel to lean forward, and takes her top off, then helps her put her pyjama top on.
Suki and Mel then slide her up the bed, roll her onto her other side, and make her comfortable with pillows, placing one between her knees, and one under her ankle so that her heels are not touching the bed, then cover her back up.
"All done, Aunty!" Suki says, and we take off our gloves and aprons, and put them in the bag with the dirty pad in, ready to take out to the bin upon leaving. Mel puts the laundry in the kitchen basket outside the room, and rejoins us.
"So that's Mrs Patel's tea time call," Suki says, taking the Care Plan folder and beginning to write notes. She sits down on the sofa and motions for me to do the same.
"Mel, what time did we log in?" Suki says.
"Twenty two minutes past three", Mel replies.
"OK, so we can leave at three forty-seven," Suki says, and fills out the notes.
"This is a half hour call, but we are allowed to leave after twenty five minutes, because on the old contracts we never had travel time, so we used to use the five minutes to get to the next call. They give us five minutes travel time now, but because we're still on the old system, we still get paid for half an hour after twenty five minutes. Plus we get to finish earlier." Mel tells me.
"You're on the new contract, though, so you'll get paid by the minute, won't you?" Suki asks me.

"Yeah, something like that!" I reply.

"Have you got your shadowing paperwork with you?" she asks.

"Yes, here you go," I say, and give it to her. She scribbles the client details and what I have observed.

"Two minutes", Mel says, looking at her phone. I put my biker jacket on and pick up my helmet, ready to leave.

"I bet its a nightmare having to take all that on and off for every call!" Suki says, looking at my helmet and backpack.

"Yeah it can be," I say, "but I can't afford a car, so it'll have to do for now!"

"I bet your petrol is cheaper, though. How many miles do you get per gallon?" she asks me.

"I get about one hundred, more if I'm economical. Stop-starting like this, though, about one hundred," I say.

"Damn, I only get thirty three!" Mel laughs, picking up the phone to log out.

"Yeah, but you have a roof it it rains, and heaters, and a boot!" I laugh.

"True!" Mel says, "do you want to follow me to the next call?"

"Yes, I'll follow", I say, walking outside and sticking my helmet on.

Over the next 7 calls, I meet Mr Kaur, Mrs Rana, and Mrs Singh who all speak Punjabi and very little English (Suki assures me that on this run, I will always be with someone Asian who can speak Punjabi), and Mr Jones, Mrs Shipway, then we go back to Mrs Rana, and Mrs Singh.

It seems to be a fairly easy run, with only 8 client calls, fairly easy tasks, and each one is a double up so I'd have company, plus each call seems to take less than twenty minutes and there was plenty time to drink my coffee.
I say goodnight to Suki and Mel, and ride round the corner to have a cigarette and my last cup of coffee from my flask.
I look at tonight's rota of 8 calls.
That was 4 hours of work, and 35 minutes of travel time.
But we finished it in 4 hours because of leaving each call after 25 minutes, so that's 35 minutes pay I'm down already.
I'd put my availability as 3pm till 11pm. 8 hours to work. And I got 4 hours of work.
I look at Thursday's rota. 11 client calls, two of them 15 minute calls. That's 5 hours of work tomorrow night.
Sunday looks better, with it being a full day, but still, out of 16 hours, I've got 5 hours in the morning, starting at 6.30 and finishing at 12pm including travel time, then I'm not back out till 16.40, finishing at 22.00, so another 5 hours plus travel time.
This week I will only be working 19 hours!
I am going to be so fucking poor. I just hope I get some more work next week!
I put my cigarette out and head home.
I arrive 10 minutes later.
This is nice, finishing on time and everything!
I started work at 15.20, and I'm home at 19.40.
Pete is surprised to see me back so soon.
"How did it go?" he asks me, giving me a cuddle as I walk through the door.

"It went quite well. I can now say 'stand up' in Punjabi!" I say, and he laughs.
"How do you say it?" he asks.
"Well, it sounds like, 'Otto!'", I tell him.
"Great stuff!" he says, "so what are the other staff like that you've met?"
"They were nice. I met Suki and Mel tonight, both really lovely, explaining things really well and quite laid back. They were really relaxed, which I think is a good sign", I tell him.
"Sounds promising!" he says, taking my jacket and hanging it up.
"Yeah, only thing is, I worked out that I'll only be doing nineteen hours this week!" I say.
"OK, well I'm sure it'll be more next week! They promised you forty four, remember. Its probably just for the shadow shifts or something!" he replies.
"Its a zero hours contract, though, honey, they don't legally have to give me any hours at all!" I respond.
"I know, but I'm sure it'll work out, honey, try not to stress!" he says.
I will try not to stress when I have to explain to my landlord that I can't pay them this month.
Yep.
Life.
Oh well.

It is Thursday, and I'm with Jaspreet tonight on a single call run.
She told me earlier on the phone to meet her at 15.40 outside Mrs Nicholls' house in Merry Hill.
She and I both arrive at 15.30.

"Hi Rose, I'm Jaspreet, but everyone calls me Jazz. Let's go inside." she says, and walks ahead to open the key safe, and unlocks the front door.

As soon as we're inside, she uses the phone to log in, then we put our gloves and aprons on, and I follow her to the living room.

"Hi Gill, this is Rose, she's new!" Jazz shouts to the client, who looks up from her armchair.

"Hello!" Gill says in a croaky voice.

"Hi there, Gill!" I say, smiling.

Gill looks at me with confusion.

"You have to shout, because she's very hard of hearing, OK?" Jazz tells me.

"Hi Gill!" I shout, and she smiles at me.

The television is blaring loudly, and Jazz takes the remote to turn it down.

"What would you like for tea, Gill?" Jazz shouts to her.

"Is there any tuna, Jasmine?" Gill asks.

"I'll go and look", she says, and beckons me to follow her to the kitchen.

She looks in the fridge, then the cupboard and takes out a tin of tuna.

"I've told Gill plenty times my name is Jaspreet, or Jazz, but she keeps calling me Jasmine anyway, so I just let her, now," she says, smiling, "everyone knows its me that she's referring to when she asks other carers how Jasmine is. She tells them all I'm her favourite!"

She walks back to the lounge and I follow.

"Gill, there's this tuna. Do you want it on a sandwich or something?" she shouts to Gill.

"Yes, with some mayonnaise, please. And a cup of tea." Gill replies.

205

"Coming up!" Jazz shouts.

We go back into the kitchen and Jazz shows me where everything is kept, and shows me where her medication is.

I put the kettle on and make the cup of tea while Jazz makes the sandwich.

"I always do the washing up here, as this is a very simple call for half an hour, but there is loads of time to do everything, and Gill likes to keep everything tidy. There isn't any washing up now, but later when we come for her bedtime call, we'll do it then", she tells me.

Jazz gets a glass of water and puts a concoction of tablets into an egg cup, and takes them through to Gill. I carry the tea and sandwich and place them on her table beside her armchair.

"Gill, can you take your medicine please?" Jazz shouts.

"Yes," Gill says, and takes the egg cup from Jazz. She then pours the tablets into her mouth, takes a sip of water, and swallows the lot in one go.

"Sit down, Rose," Jazz says, and we sit on the sofa opposite Gill. Jazz takes the Care Plan folder and writes some notes in it, and signs off the medication on the chart.

"I usually stay between twenty five and twenty seven minutes in these calls," Jazz tells me, "so we can leave in eight minutes".

"OK," I say, and see Gill tucking into her sandwich, watching the TV.

"This is our last call tonight, so do you want to leave your bike on the drive and come in my car to save time?" she asks.

"Yes please", I reply, "it'll be nice to be inside for a change!"

Jazz continues writing notes, then puts the folder away.

She looks at my shadowing paperwork and fills it out with brief details.

We say goodbye to Gill, and I chuck my helmet, bag and jacket on the back seats, then climb into the passenger's seat.

Jazz drives us to the next client, Mr Scott.

Mr Scott barely speaks to us, just grunts and stares at the TV.

In this call, I make a chicken and salad sandwich for him, and Jazz washes up and makes him a coffee.

Jazz applies Dermol cream to his lower legs and feet, and I fill out the paperwork.

Next, we visit Lorna, who is a very chatty and energetic wheelchair user, who has a black cat called Tom. Jazz shows me where everything is, and we help Lorna onto the commode, change her pad, help her off the commode and into her armchair.

Then we make her a cheese and salad sandwich, feed the cat, wash up, make her a cuppa, empty and clean out the commode, and sit down for a quick chat about cats while filling out the paperwork.

"I hate cats", Jazz says on our way back to her car.

"Really?" I ask.

"Yes, I can't stand them. Lorna's cat just hisses at me whenever I go by it. They don't like me and I don't like them!" she tells me.

"I love cats", I tell her.

She says nothing.

We get through the next 7 calls quickly and efficiently, with Jazz showing me where everything is kept, and how everyone likes their tea and coffee, and talking me through what clients are like, which clients have mood swings, which clients play up and don't want to go to bed, etc.

We arrive back at Gill's for our last call, so I take my belongings inside with us.

Gill very slowly makes her way to the toilet upon our arrival. Whilst she's in there, Jazz talks me through her bedtime routine.

"She always goes to the toilet when we get here, so when she's in there, we make her a cup of cocoa, turn everything off in the lounge, close all the curtains, put the bedside lamp on, pull back the covers for her, then help her into her nightie and tuck her in".

"OK," I say, following her into the kitchen.

I wash up while Jazz makes the cocoa, then we go into the bedroom, and Jazz puts the drink on the bedside table for her and pulls back the covers. I close the curtains, and then Gill very slowly walks in to us.

Jazz helps her to undress, and I pass her the nightie, then fold the clothes and place them on a chair as requested by Gill.

Once she's tucked up in bed, we close the door, leaving it ajar slightly, then go back in the lounge, turning everything off except the light, which we leave on so that Jazz can write out the notes.

"How have you found tonight?" she asks me.

"It's been quite good," I tell her, "really straightforward compared to what I'm used to".

"Have you done Community Care before?" she asks.

"Yes, for a different company. It was very hectic. We've done eleven calls tonight, and we're finishing early in the same area we started work in. At my last place, we'd have eleven calls, but they'd all be miles apart from each other, and you'd finish ten miles away from your house, running late all night!" I say.

"They are quite good here, they keep you in the same area all shift, with the same clients, so you know when you will finish." Jazz says.

She finishes writing, and puts the folder down.

"Do you want to get your things together? It's time to go now," Jazz says, standing up.

I grab my kit, put my jacket on, and walk towards the door.

Jazz turns off the lights behind us and calls goodnight to Gill.

She locks up and puts the key back in the key safe.

"OK, goodnight Rose. See you again!" Jazz says, and gets in her car.

"Night, Jazz!" I reply, and she speeds off down the road before I've even put my helmet on.

Jazz seems nice, but she doesn't talk much. She hasn't been unpleasant at all, I've just sensed all shift that I've been holding her up or something, because she's so quick at doing things, whereas I'm learning where things are and what to do in the calls, and quite a few times she's taken over from me to speed things up.

Never mind.

I am finishing my shift at 20.40, and I arrive home at 20.52.

Not bad at all.
But it is bad, because I'm gonna have hardly any money this month.
I didn't sign up for part time.

I call Paula, my Coordinator, on Friday morning, to ask her if I can do any more shadowing this week. She says that there's no point as after Sunday I'll have shadowed all of the calls on these runs, but she assures me she's got shadow shifts set up for me next week in different areas.
Friday and Saturday I spend doing laundry and spending time with Pete, working on our motorbikes.

Sunday comes, and I head out to start my shift and meet Kelly at 6.30am on the dot. Kelly tells me that Lydia is off sick today, so she will be covering her shift, and I'll be with her all day today.
Kelly is nice and chatty, and talks me through today's run, saying that there's a couple of difficult clients on it, where it is pretty much impossible to please them, but other than that, it should be plain sailing.
Kelly also works for their other branch based in Cannock, and tells me that they cover areas in Staffordshire, and tells me to try there to pick up extra shifts, as things are a bit slow in Wolverhampton at the moment.
I decide that I will. I need the hours.
"Chuck your things in my boot, and then you can jump in with me, it'll be quicker," Kelly tells me, opening her boot for me.

"Thanks," I say, and place my helmet, bag and jacket inside.

I follow Kelly up the garden path to our first client's house, and she shows me where the key safe is, and then unlocks the door.

The first thing that hits us as we go in, is a stale fishy smell.

Kelly logs in on the phone, and I follow her upstairs, putting my gloves and apron on.

"Morning, Josie!", she calls, knocking the bedroom door before entering.

Josie opens her eyes slowly, and reaches out of the covers to switch the lamp on.

"Oh no, not you!", Josie says, smiling at kelly.

"Tough luck, Josie, you're stuck with me today!" Kelly says, and smiles back, "plus, we've got a new carer, Rose, who is starting with us!"

Josie looks me up and down, and says, "good morning, dear!"

"Morning!" I reply.

Kelly supports Josie's back as she sits up, then pulls the bed sheets back, swings her feet out, and slides her slippers on.

"OK, Rose, so we're gonna help Josie onto the toilet in the bathroom, and give her a wash, then help her to get dressed. Are you OK to help her get undressed while I fetch her clean clothes and make the bed?" Kelly asks me, as Josie stands up, takes her walking frame and heads towards the upstairs bathroom.

"Yes, sure," I say, and follow Josie.

I put my gloves and apron on, and help her take her knickers down. She then sits on the toilet.

"Would you like some privacy?" I ask her, heading out of the door.

"No, my love, just help me off with my nightie, then run the hot tap in the sink," she says, "I'll tell you what you gotta do, don't you worry!" she says, and laughs.

I smile and do as I'm told.

"Put a bit of that soapy stuff on a flannel," she says, pointing at a bottle of shower gel, "dip it in the water, and then you can start washing my back if you like".

"OK," I say, following her instructions, and pass her another flannel so that she can wash her face.

Kelly comes in with the clean clothes and lies them over the bath.

"Josie, are you happy for Rose to carry on with your wash and help you get dressed, while I make your breakfast?" Kelly asks her.

"Yes, you carry on, my love, we've got it all under control!" she says, giggling.

"You OK with that, Rose?" Kelly asks me.

"Yes, no problem!" I reply, drying Josie's back with a towel.

I hear Kelly going downstairs, and carry on washing Josie's arms and torso, and drying her off.

I then pass her her deodorant spray as requested, which she uses and hands me back, then I help her to put her bra, top and cardigan on.

Josie stands up and I wash her legs, groin and bottom for her, then dry her off.

She applies some talc powder to her inner thighs, then sits down again, and I help her on with her knickers, trousers, socks and slippers.

She then stands up again, and I pull her clothes up over the waist, tucking in her top.
I empty the sink and Josie cleans her teeth, while I flush the toilet and pick up the laundry to take downstairs.
Kelly comes back up and sets the stair lift up ready for Josie to sit in, and Josie asks me to brush her hair for her.
I do this, and then put a plait in her pony tail for her, tying it off with a hair elastic.
She put her glasses on, and then walks over with her frame to the stair lift to sit down.
"Have you done my porridge?" she asks Kelly, as we descend the stairs ahead of her.
"Yes, with some strawberries", Kelly replies.
"And my cup of coffee?" she asks Kelly.
"Yes, Josie, with two sugars", Kelly says, rolling her eyes and smiling as she puts the walking frame in front of the stair lift.
"And have you put them on the table my my chair?" Josie asks.
"Yes, Josie, and I've put the gas fire on, too, and put the news on the telly ready for you!" Kelly says, and laughs.
Josie laughs too, as she stands up and walks into her lounge.
"I like things to be done the way I like", Josie says to me, as she sits down in her arm chair and lifts up her feet.
Kelly pushes a footstool underneath for her.
"That's fair enough," I tell her, taking off my gloves and apron, and putting them in the kitchen bin.
"I'll have my tablets today," she tells Kelly.
Kelly takes a glass of water and an egg cup with tablets to Josie, who picks them out one

by one, places them in her mouth, and swallows them with a sip of water.

"All gone!", Josie says, "I'll be good today!"

"Thank you!" Kelly says, laughing, and takes the egg cup into the kitchen, then comes back and sits down on the sofa, and begins to fill out the care notes.

"Josie doesn't always take her medication," Kelly tells me, "because the side effects of some of the tablets is nausea and dizziness, and so she sometimes refuses".

"Oh, OK", I say.

"Always ask her first if she wants them, because if you get them out and she doesn't want them, you have to go on a trip to the pharmacy to give them to dispose of safely. She'll usually tell you if she wants them or not, but always check, and fill out the In-discrepancy form behind the medication chart if she doesn't have them." Kelly tells me.

We leave Josie watching TV with her breakfast, and head off to the next client.

We assist 2 gentlemen and 3 ladies getting washed and dressed, give 4 sets of medication, make 5 breakfasts, feed 2 pets, put 2 loads of laundry on, then have a late cancellation when we arrive to a client who is just going out with his family to lunch.

We now have 35 minutes to kill.

"My house is just a few streets away, so I'm thinking of popping by to grab something to eat. Do you want to come?" Kelly asks me as we get back into her car.

"Erm, yes OK, if you're sure?" I reply.

"Yeah it's fine, I'm not gonna go home and leave you stranded! Come and have a coffee!" she says, and so we head over to hers.
Kelly tells me to have a seat in the kitchen and sticks the kettle on.
"Do you want some toast? I'm making some", she says.
"No, I'm OK thanks, but I'll just nip outside for a cigarette if that's alright," I reply.
She takes an ashtray from the window ledge and passes it to me.
"You can smoke in here, it's fine, my mom does," she tells me.
"Thank you", I say, and light one up.
She plonks a coffee in front of me, butters some toast, and sits down opposite me at the table to eat it.
"You've done care work before, haven't you?" she asks me between mouthfuls.
"Yeah, a few months in the community, and six weeks in a home. i didn't like the home, though, I prefer to do this," I tell her, blowing smoke behind me.
"I've never worked in a care home before, but I know carers who have, and none of them liked it, really, and came to community work", she says, "I guess its better to work with people in the comfort of their own homes."
"I think so," I tell her, "for me it was just being stuck in the same place with bored residents who I barely had time to speak to. The ones who didn't have dementia so bad they didn't know where they were, were bored out of their minds, staring at the television all day long with nothing to do".
I take a sip of my coffee.

"I don't think I'd like it," she says, "I like being able to come home when I'm on a break!"

"I guess it's good living so close to where you're working!" I reply.

She nods and starts on her second slice of toast.

"I like being able to have a couple minutes to myself between clients if I'm having a bad day. There's a lot more freedom in this, with no managers breathing down your neck all the while. You can just get on with your work at your own pace. There seems to be enough time to chat with clients with this firm. At my last company they were always telling us to cut calls short and we were always running late, it was so stressful!" I tell her.

"They are quite good here, to be fair. I do admin at the office in Cannock in the mornings, then do a few shifts on the evening or at weekends. We don't usually run late, to be fair. When we do, its because someone has died or is really ill or something. It's pretty well organised, and carers who have been here for ages swap their calls round to run more efficiently, and most of the time we finish early. Like, we'll be done by twelve, but then on the evening run we'll finish at around half eight, nine at the latest" Kelly says, and finishes her toast.

"It says ten o'clock finish on the rota!" I say, surprised.

"Yes, but we'll only stay twenty-five minutes in the half hour calls, shave some time off the travel time, and finish early. You'll see!" she says.

We both pop to the toilet, then head back out to the last call - a quick 15 minute job, of giving tablets, making a cup of tea and a sandwich, a scribble in the care notes, and then she drops me by my bike.
I grab my kit and warm up the engine.
"Meet me back here at half four! See you later!" she shouts from the open car window, and drives off.
I head home, make some noodles, do a load of laundry, wash up the dishes, drink some coffee, watch some TV with Pete, smoke a couple cigarettes, then head back out to meet Kelly.

I chuck my stuff into Kelly's car boot, and we go back to see Josie.
This call, we heat a microwave meal up for her, give her some tablets, make her a coffee and wash up dishes in the kitchen, then sit down to write care notes and watch a quiz show with her for ten minutes.
Next, we go to see a gentleman named John, who follows us, shuffling around as we wash up dishes, hang up his laundry and heat his ready meal for him, complaining that the other carers don't do it properly.
Kelly asks him if he wants to make a complaint, but he declines.
We serve him his meal and his cup of tea, then listen to him complain some more - this time about the neighbours cutting a hedge - and then fill out the care notes, and leave him to it.
"He's one of the difficult ones I told you about earlier. Today he hasn't been too bad, but

sometimes you'll go and he'll be in a right mood, following you around and critisizing your every action, putting dishes back in the sink that you've just washed up, and just moaning!" Kelly tells me on the way to our next client.

Next we see Beverley, a West Indian lady, who tells us that none of the carers have been to her today. Kelly checks the care notes, and tells her politely that she's mistaken.

"Bev has dementia, and forgets. She also thinks that when we go, another carer will come, like on shifts. She gets funny when you try to leave, so just be warned!" Kelly tells me in the kitchen as we prepare her soup and medication.

Once Kelly logs out on the phone and we get up to leave, Bev gets up.

"You can't go, the other one not arrived yet!" she says.

"We'll be back later, Bev!" Kelly tells her, "it will be around seven o'clock. We have to go to someone else, now!"

"You don't like me, that's what it is!" Bev says. We head towards the door.

"Yes we do, Bev, we'll be back later!" Kelly assures her, and nods for me to go outside.

We go outside and Bev locks the door behind us, but we can hear her shouting something about us being racist and not liking her.

In the car, Kelly says, "she can be funny with you at times, it depends what kind of mood she's in. She's lovely, but very insecure, so she needs lots of reassurance. But when your time's up, go, because she'll keep you there all day, otherwise."

"OK, I'll try and remember that!" I reply.
We fly through the next five calls, making ready meals, sandwiches, drinks, giving medication, washing up, folding laundry and taking one client to bed.
Last call is Josie, where we started.
We give her her medication, make her a hot chocolate and help her into bed, then wash up, fill out the notes, switch the lights and the gas fire off, and leave.
"Thanks for today", I say to Kelly as I grab my kit out of her car.
"No problem, you've done really well!" she says, "see you round! Goodnight!" she calls.
"Goodnight!" I reply, and she drives off.
I look at my phone. It is 20.33. Early finish as predicted.
It has started to rain, so I throw my jacket, bag and helmet on, and set off home, too.
I purchase two pizzas on the way back for Pete and I, and once home, we eat them in bed watching a DVD, until I fall asleep.

Monday. I call into the office to see Paula and collect this week's rotas, and some more boxes of gloves.
She gives me three rotas. Tonight, Thursday and Sunday. She tells me there isn't any more shadowing in Wolverhampton to do after I've done these.
Tonight I'll be with Jazz on a double up run with Goldthorn and Parkfields clients,
Thursday I'll be with Paula on a double up run in Wednesfield and Low Hill, then on Sunday it will be the Pendeford run with Kelly again.

On the way back to my bike, I light a cigarette in the car park and call the Cannock office to see if I can do any shadowing with them on their Staffordshire runs.
I speak with Penny, their Coordinator, who asks if I'd like to do the Penkridge run.
I tell her I will, as I'm very familiar with Penkridge, and agree to do a shadow shift on Wednesday evening. She says I'll be with Kelly on that run, as she covers Penkridge and Cannock, and just helps out with the Wolverhampton branch when they're short staffed.
Sorted.

I head out to meet Jazz at the first call on tonight's run, and meet Abi, the other carer on the double up.
Jazz and Abi get out of their cars and begin speaking to each other in Punjabi, and laughing.
"Hello, Rose, I'm Abi", Abi says, walking past me to open the key safe.
"Hello, Rose", Jazz says, following her.
Abi logs them both in on the phone upon entering, and we all put our gloves and aprons on.
We go in to Mr Champa, who is in the lounge.
"Hello, Uncle", Jazz says, pulling the hoist out as Abi grabs the sling and slides it behind Mr Champa's back.
"Hello Mr Champa, I'm Rose", I say to him, smiling.
He looks at me and nods.
"OK Rose, can you get the commode and bring it here?" Jazz says.

I see it at the other end of the room and bring it over, locking the brakes.

Abi speaks to Mr Champa in Punjabi.

"She's just telling him that he is going onto the commode", Jazz tells me, as she operates the hoist to lift him up, then down onto the commode seat.

Once he's down, Abi leaves the room, and Jazz sits down to start writing the care notes.

Abi comes back after 5 minutes, and speaks to Mr Champa again.

"He says he's finished", Abi tells us.

Jazz gets up and operates the hoist to lift him up.

"Nothing", Abi tells her, looking in the empty bowl.

"OK, we'll get him seated", Jazz says, moving the hoist over to the chair, then lowering him, with Abi guiding the sling.

Once he's comfortable, Abi covers him with a blanket, and they sit down on the sofa again, speaking to each other in Punjabi, laughing.

Mrs Champa comes into the room and sits in the armchair next to her husband, and starts knitting.

"Hello, Aunty!" Jazz says, and all three have a conversation in Punjabi, not bothering to try to include me or explain what they are talking about, which I feel a little rude, to be honest.

"Rose, get your things together and start your bike, we're leaving in a minute", Jazz tells me.

I get kitted up and start the bike as Jazz and Abi rush out, jump into their cars and speed off.

I try to follow Jazz, but lose her at an island and can't see where she's turned off.

Great.

I pull over when I can, get my satnav and the rota out, and type in the address for the next call.

I go there.

They haven't even waited for me, they've just left the door open for me.

I go in, and both of them are already sorting out Mrs Nagra.

"Rose, go in the kitchen, and make a cup of warm milk in the microwave. Its the door at the end of the hall", Jazz says without looking at me.

Without apologising for driving off and leaving me.

I'm feeling quite pissed off right now.

I go and do as asked.

When I come back and place the drink on the table, Abi hands me the commode pot full of sloppy shit and urine mixed with toilet paper.

"Can you empty this and clean it out, Rose? The bathroom is next to the kitchen on the right", she says.

Again, I go and do it, and come back to the living room, where they are all now sat, chattering away in Punjabi, and showing each other things on their phones.

"In the next few calls, can you please talk me through the calls, so I know what I'm doing when I'm out on this run? I'd like to be quite hands on, too", I say to Jazz.

"No problem", she replies, and goes back to her conversation with Abi while Mrs Nagra watches TV.

Again, Jazz tells me to get kitted up before they've left, and again they both speed off in their cars.

This time, I speed behind them, making sure I keep up.

When we arrive, they're both going inside before I've taken my helmet off and leave the door open.

Jazz tells me to jump in the car with her after this one and lock my bike up, as this client is also our last call.

During the next 5 client calls, I feel more and more irritated that I don't know what's being said by or to the clients, and Jazz and Abi seem intent to just rush through the calls because it's quicker than when I am assisting.

"I'm slower than you guys because I don't know these calls. It would help a lot if you could talk me through them and explain what is being said, because I don't understand Punjabi, and if the client doesn't understand English, it's going to be difficult to communicate with them," I say to Jazz in the car.

"Don't worry, you'll pick it up in the calls. Abi and I work fast. All we say to clients is what we're doing, and a bit of chit chat", Jazz says.

At the last client call, I get out of the car and knock the front door for the client's wife to let us in.

Jazz walks in first.

"Rose, is it your things on the pavement?" Abi asks me.

I look behind me, and see that Jazz has taken my helmet, jacket and backpack out of her car and left them on the pavement out in the street.

What the fuck!

My £100 helmet with my £50 gloves inside, my £70 jacket, and my backpack with my purse, house keys, and client address lists in. On the side of the fucking road!

Who does that?

If she wanted me to get my stuff out of the car, why didn't she just say? I would have happily taken it out with me.

And she actually put it on the pavement. Why didn't she carry it over with her?

I drop my things in the client's hallway next to the radiator, and go into the back room where the client is.

Jazz and Abi do the call by themselves. I get the task of taking the soiled rubbish out while they continue to speak in Punjabi and make no effort to explain what is being said, and don't seem interested in talking me through the call.

I give up asking, now.

I'm surprised at jazz, though, as I thought that we got along OK the last time I worked with her. She seems off with me, now.

"How come you left my things on the pavement? If you'd said you wanted them out of your car, I would have took them inside with me", I say to Jazz.

"I'm going to go straight home from here, so I took them out. I thought you'd seen them", she says, then carries on her conversation with Abi.

No apology.

She clearly thinks that leaving someone's belongings on the street is perfectly acceptable because she wants to rush off.
Grr.
Smile, Rose, you're in the presence of a client, and you're at work.
Stay professional.
There's a good girl.

I get home, still feeling annoyed with Jazz. I tell Pete about it, and he agrees that it was rude to speak to each other and to clients in another language and not tell me what was being said.
It's not like I want a full translation, just the gist of it.
And I want to be trained when I'm out supposedly on training, not being pushed aside so that they can rush off.
And leaving my stuff in the street? Not happy.
Didn't like that shift at all.
I have a glass of wine, and relax a little, with Pete giving me a shoulder rub.
We make love, and then fall asleep.

It is Tuesday, and I have a day off.
Normally I'd be happy about it, but I'm not, because I can't afford to pay my bills on so little hours.
I've had my Universal Credit payment of only £162, and next week, when I get my first pay from my new job, I'll have an additional £341 for the 44 hours I'll have done over the last 2 weeks.
Usually, I'd pick up £300 in one week.

Massive reduction in wages due to lack of hours.
This month, I'll have a total of £503.
My rent is £525.
Fucking hell.
I need to also put fuel in my bike so I can actually get to work.
And I need to pay my loan, council tax, electric, phone, and eat.
Great.
I'm in the shit this month.
Like I said, I was promised 44 hours a week at interview.
It was bullshit, clearly.
Things are 'a bit slow', Paula said, as so many clients died and they haven't replaced them.
Kelly had mentioned that they weren't getting any more clients yet as the Wolverhampton branch was about to be bought out by another and they weren't sure who yet, so they weren't allowed to take on any more clients.
So it looks like I've joined a company headed for the shitter.
I can't afford to work here.
I need to find another job, and it's only week 2.
I will end up homeless at this rate!
I spend today applying for jobs, absolutely any kind of jobs - warehousing, front of house, cleaning, etc - apart from care work.
Care Work is so difficult.
I've learned that I don't want to work in a care home again. I hated it.
Domiciliary care, in the community, is underpaid, as you can work a 70 hour week driving around in all weathers, and only get

paid for maybe 40 - 50 hours, and end up earning below the minimum wage.

For a job that requires so much responsibility, dedication and accuracy, receiving minimum wage is a fucking joke, let's face it.

Give dear old Betty the wrong tablets at lunch time, she could be dead by tea time.

Since starting care work, my finances have gotten progressively worse. It just does not pay.

If you only have 1 wage coming in like I do, it is almost impossible to stay afloat and keep putting fuel into a vehicle to continue earning less and less.

I just can't do this anymore.

It is decided.

Wednesday's run in Penkridge with Kelly is only 4 hours work, with 8 client calls, and all calls are nice and easy.

All of the clients go to the toilet themselves, just require assistance getting dressed for bed, meal preparation and medications.

Really, fucking easy run.

I've even got a familiar client from my old company, Jackie, who changed care providers after I left, so I'm pleased, as I've always gotten on really well with her. She's the most independent 95 year old I've ever met, and now I actually have time to sit and have coffee with her.

Great stuff!

Kelly signs off my shadowing form and says she'll hand it into the office tomorrow.

I go home after only a 4 hour shift, but at least it's a shift.

Thursday, and I'm with Paula and a lovely Asian lady called Sabi, who speaks with the most common Black Country accent in English, then switches into a heavily accented Punjabi with a couple of the clients.
She also explains what she's saying, which I like.
They are both really easy people to work with. I jump in the car with both of them, and they both give me a run down of the each client's call on route to them, so I know what to expect before going in, and they actually let me get stuck in and be hands on.
I'm using hoists, helping undress and dress clients, chatting to clients, fill out care notes, getting medication ready under full supervision (which nobody else has let me do so far), and then they take me to KFC mid shift.
"Aren't we going to be late?" I ask, eating my chicken in the car with them.
"No, we'll be finished by half nine", Paula says, "when you're as used to this run as us, you'll fly through it".
And they are not wrong.
We finish the last call at 21.30 and I head home, having really enjoyed my shift.
It makes all the difference when you get to work with good people.

Sunday's shift goes smoothly with Kelly. Kelly pretty much lets me do everything myself while she supervises and makes drinks and helps tidy up.

Because these are all single calls and there's two of us, the workload is halved so we spend extra time chatting with the clients, making jokes and looking through photo albums, and get lots of coffee.
It is nice to be able to work at a relaxed pace.
If I could get enough hours, I would stay with this company.
I just can't afford to.
We get a 2 hour break after the lunch calls, then meet back up for the teas and bed times, and we finish at 20.47.
I get home and have a look at the rotas for next week which have been posted out to me.
I've got 4 double up calls in Goldthorn on Tuesday (2 hours), and a full day on Sunday, with only a 45 minute gap (10 hours).
12 fucking hours. I need another 32!
Damn it!

Monday, I call up Penny at the Cannock office.
She gives me the Penkridge run on Wednesday and Thursday and says she'll post the rotas out to me first class so I should get them tomorrow.
2 shifts, but only another 8 hours work, bringing this week's total to 20 hours.
I also get an email back from a gardening company I've applied to, after a tip off from a friend who does casual labour for them.
Looks like I've got a job interview tomorrow morning.
Yay!
It's at 10am so I'll have plenty time to get back for my 2 hour shift in the evening.

I've also had an email from a cleaning job I applied for, which is full time at a mental health hospital. I have an interview on Wednesday, too.
Excellent!
I'm gonna get me some hours.

Tuesday's interview with the gardening company goes well, I think. The boss doesn't give a lot away. If anything, he looks like he wants to escape the room the entire time and seems anxious, while his mother who works there asks most of the questions and I make her laugh a lot with my cheeky answers and jokes.
I am told by the boss that he'll let me know by the end of the week.
Ok.
Pete has been waiting outside for me, and he takes me for a quick coffee on the way back to discuss how it went.
I then go to work to see 4 clients, with Jazz as my double up carer.
She continues rushing off in her car without waiting for me, and sighing when I take my time making sure I'm doing everything properly, because I'm not familiar with these clients, and I like to chat to my clients while I'm working, to help put them at ease.
She is very impatient with me, and rushes off in her car after my 4th call, with just an abrupt "see you" as a goodbye.
I go home and pour Pete and I a glass of wine. He buys us a Chinese takeaway and we watch a film in bed, having a cuddle and eating our food.

Wednesday's cleaning interview doesn't go well at all.

I've got more years of experience than they wanted, plus a cleaning NVQ and recent COSHH training, and I'm familiar with working with people with mental health issues, due to my current job.

I had even researched the company.

The interviewers seem disinterested, and ask me questions, using abbreviations.

"Do you know much about PFC?" one of them ask me, right after we'd been talking about COSHH and health and safety.

I assumed she was on about another regulation or something.

"No, I can't say I've heard of it", I reply.

The interviewers look at each other, and the other one says, "Passion For Care is a well established company who run many centres like this one across the country, and what we do is specialise in providing mental health care for young adults".

"Oh, right," I reply, "I did actually research the company. If you'd said 'Passion For Care' I could have told you what I knew. I thought you were referring to some kind of regulation like COSHH".

They look at each other again.

I know now that I haven't got this job.

At this point, I don't even want it anymore.

You know sometimes when you can just tell straight away that someone doesn't like you? Yeah, well, that's the vibes I'm getting sat in this room with these two women.

Once I've been seen out, I wander down the driveway and light a cigarette, and call Pete to let him know I'm ready for him.
He's been sat in a cafe having coffee.
"How did it go?" he asks, pulling up next to me.
"Shit, but sod it!" I say, "they were bitches in the interview, and one of them would have been my boss, so I don't want to work there anyway!"
Pete laughs.
I put my helmet on and climb onto the back of his bike.
We go home and have some lunch, and then I head out to work in Penkridge.
I enjoy my nice, easy run of simple calls with nice, chatty clients, and I'm home by 9pm.

Thursday, I clean mine and Pete's bikes while he stays in bed watching TV, and then I do 2 loads of laundry, have some toast, and go to work for my Penkridge run again.
Come 9pm I'm home, and I have 2 days off now to relax.

Friday, I have an email from the gardening company, stating that they wish to offer me the job.
Yes!
Great stuff!
I'm supposed to give one month's notice according to my contract, but I could start my new job in 2 weeks.
I pop into the office to go and speak with Paula in person.

I tell her that I've had to look for another job, as even with working for both Wolverhampton and Cannock, I'm simply not getting enough work to cover my bills, and ask if I can give 2 weeks instead.
She assures me it's fine and apologises that she can't offer me any more work.
Awesome.
I confirm with my new boss that I'll be able to start with them in a fortnight.
I feel quite excited and relieved.
Then I call the bank to tell them that I can't afford to make my loan payment this month, and explain my circumstances - that I can't pay my rent or any of my bills of buy groceries for a week - and assure them that my circumstances are about to change for the better soon.
They agree to stop my payments for 2 months, and then have another look at my finances to see where I'm at.
My electric company agrees another payment plan with me to clear my £300 arrears.
But it is all going to be OK, I'm hoping.
I will have a steady income again, with set work hours, and no more shifts.
I am going to sort my shit out.
I am.

Over the next two weeks, I have 8 shifts ranging from 6 client calls (3 hours) to full day's shifts on Sundays (10 hours). I still don't do more than 24 hours a week, even picking up shifts with the Cannock branch.

I finish my last shift on a Sunday at 21.00, and get home in the dark.
I feel really, really relieved.
No more care work for me!
And it feels so GOOD!
I have learned so much from this line of work, and I will never forget it. I will forever appreciate all of the hard work that Care staff do.
Working in Care has tested me beyond all of my limits, and pushed me so close to the edge that there were a couple of times that I almost fell off.
Having a partner helped, to have someone to keep me grounded and reason with me when I was prepared to go out on shift when I could barely stay awake or was feeling rough and too exhausted.
If I had been single, I do believe that I would have continued plodding on a few times, and maybe ended up being one of those carers who crashed their vehicles due to extreme exhaustion, or fucking up someone's medication and putting others' lives at risk.
I have learnt so much about myself, too, like how much I can actually handle, thinking on my feet constantly, and being able to keep a smile on my face for someone else's sake when I feel like I've hit rock bottom.
Care Work isn't just about providing a service. It isn't just a job. It is SO much more than that.
Yes, we help people get about, and meet their daily practical needs, but we also bring a friendly face and a listening ear. We bring a smile, and a joke, and laughter. We bring

companionship and compassion. We are ready to deal with a crisis if need be, to call an ambulance, to keep an eye on your loved ones and make sure that they are getting the support that they need, their medication on time and three meals a day. We are a lifeline to people out in the sticks down dark country lanes whose nearest local shop is over 3 miles away, so we go and get the loaf of bread and milk, and we find the right channel on the TV, and we have a look at the fuse box when the electricity unexpectedly goes out and flick the switch in the dark garage to turn it back on, and we fold the laundry and butter the toast just how they like it.

We fill up the bird feeders so that they can sit and watch them from the window; we change light bulbs; we take the rubbish out and put the wheelie bin at the bottom of the drive when it's bin day; we change bed sheets; we collect prescriptions; we do ironing; we read the newspaper out loud; we help fill out forms and many, many other tasks which aren't always on the care plan, but we do if there's time, because we care.

We sacrifice time with our loved ones to be with your loved ones.

We are very, very tired people who are always hungry and thirsty and need a wee, and simply don't get paid enough to do what we do.

I think that it takes a very special person to stick at this job long term, and someone who isn't afraid to stick up for themselves and say, 'no, I'm not working tomorrow morning when I've just come off a night shift'.

Care is not for the fainthearted. You have to be resilient, fast thinking, and a genuinely kind and compassionate person. You have to have empathy, and be patient and understanding.

You can't just walk in to someone's home at 6am when they are sleeping, bang the light on and talk loudly, and roughly wash them down when they're not feeling well.

You have to be able to clean up someone's cabbage scented shit without heaving, or showing any kind of discomfort.

You have to be respectful, and preserve dignity at all times.

Don't leave someone's willy on show, for example. Cover it with a towel. Would you want your bits out on show when you're already feeling vulnerable?

I'm guessing not.

Close the curtains when you're helping someone get dressed.

Close the door if there are other people present in the house.

Ask them what they want, and allow them time to tell you.

These simple things are so important!

One day, I may need help from a Care Assistant.

If I ever do, I will always get the coffee and the biscuits in ready for them coming.

Enough, now.

I'm going to bed looking forward to finally having enough sleep.

Goodnight x

Printed in Great Britain
by Amazon